LOVE & ROMANCE & YOUR SOUL
Loving Him, Loving Her

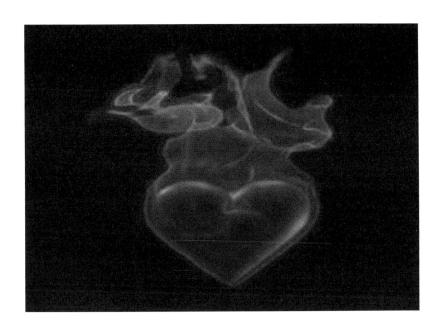

NOVEMBER 14, 2015

1ST EDITION

By Rosalind Solomon

By Rosalind Solomon

We know and hear often that love is patient and kind, not envious or prideful. We also know and hear that human's love is a reflection of divine love. We know that God is love. But how do we understand love and God Love and its work in our lives, Is its perils and rewards? Here, Rosalind Solomon looks at human love in many different facet. Through Singelness marriage. Also for the Soul and the Spirit and affection, Passionate, love that can run counter to happiness and poses real danger. As well as showing

the greatest, most spiritual, and least selfish. Proper love is a risk, but to bar oneself from it is to deny love it is a dampening choice. Love is a need and a gift; love brings joy and laughter. We must seek to be awakened and so to find an Appreciative love through

which all things are possible. And all possibility is Pure Love God is love. Rosalind Solomon is also the author of Waiting in God Waiting Room for your Godly Marriage

By Rosalind Solomon

Love is gentle

Love is kind Love

is when two lives

combine

A Poem of Love

A TRUE Godly Man

Righteousness not Compromise

Fear God, Fear not Man

Goodness and Contentment

Waiting Upon God, not Man

Faith and Faithfulness

Truth Not Deception

Love not Lusts

Love's Power over Lust | Love is God's Way

God is Love Love for Our Neighbor

Seeking God's Love Love's Mighty Touch

Love in Marriage Tough Love

Love One Another Testimonies on God's Love

Grace and Graciousness

Humble not Proud

By Rosalind Solomon

Pure Heart, not DividedWhat is The True Meaning of Love?

Dictionaries have different meanings for this word. But when I think about it, my mind conjures up images of all kinds of beautiful things that I have always associated with love. Flowers, chocolates, light dinners, hearts, clothes. These are the thing's and words that have become synonymous with love. but what about the feelings and emotions associated with it!

When I was growing up with many stars in my eyes and love songs ringing through my ears. My dreams grew bigger and I began waiting for my Prince Charming to come along and take me with him to a beautiful place where we would be surrounded by servants, good clothes, flowers and good stuff. One day I realized the truth about love that it was much more than material comforts and mere gains.

Love is Sharing

I can tell you that this is one of the most important ingredients of love. It is important to open one's heart and share your happiness, your sorrows, your fears, your victories everything, it really does not matter, as long as the heart is very clear. Love is being totally honest and knowing that the other person feels the same way too, it is sharing and losing one's inhibitions and self also knowing that the person on the other side will never be judgmental of you.

Love is Talking

Really love is, love is talking. It is about speaking, telling and sharing. After some time, people restrict their conversations to discussing bills, schooled, children and pets. This is a sure indicator of things going downhill. You have to bring the spark back by starting a conversation. Talking can help solve matters as well that otherwise might lead to misunderstandings. Another aspect of that is listening. Talking is useless if the other person is not listening. Learn to listen to it is wise to do so.

Love is Spending Time Together

By Rosalind Solomon

A few minutes spent together every day keeps the boredom away. I just made this up right now, but it is because I feel there is nothing like time invested in a relationship...believe me, it pays! Heavy work schedule takes up much time and effort, so it is important to get things into perspective. Spending time with each other will let you understand the other person better, help you know them better. And I believe that it gives the relation a different feel.

Love is Trust

When you love someone, you have to trust them. Love without trust is not possible. When you open your heart to someone, you have to trust them to take care of it, forever. Trust means that you have the confidence in the other person that they will keep their promises, be faithful and be there for you always.

Love is Faithfulness

To love means to be true, to love unconditionally means to give with all your heart to one, and only one. Being faithful in a relationship is very important, in love... it is the next thing to trust. Love is when you realize that that person is the best thing that has happened to you and you want to cherish that person and the moments spent with them, till death do you part.

Love is being best friends with each other

Love is Being Friends

Enjoying simple pleasures in one's life, like shopping, catching a movie or watching movie at home, apart from a host of other things that "Friends" normally do! You have to tell them your secrets and keep theirs, be there for each other, and respect and trust each other.

And, as clichéd as this may sound... Love is looking together in the same direction, having the same goals and taking steps in that direction to make them come true.

God loves Spiritual hunger for GOD love

What exactly are these spiritual hunger pains that we feel as we ache for more of Him? What causes this lovesickness to be awakened in our hearts? It comes from an awakened hunger that Jesus doesn't immediately satisfy. We get stirred to reach out for Him and possess Him in fullness, but the fullness has yet to be released to answer the groan within. This hunger pain forces us into deeper pursuit of His presence, of Him. This desperate agonizing yearning is how God enlarges our hearts to receive yet more of Him.

9 Bible Verses about

Being In Love1 Corinthians 13:4

Love is patient, love is kind and is not jealous; love does not brag and is not arrogant,

John 3:16

"For God so loved the world, that He gave His only begotten Son, that whoever believes in Him shall not perish, but have eternal life.

1 John 4:8

The one who does not love does not know God, for God is love.

Proverbs 10:12

Hatred stirs up strife, But love covers all transgressions.

Proverbs 17:17

A friend loves at all times, And a brother is born for adversity.

Jeremiah 31:3

The LORD appeared to him from afar, saying, "I have loved you with an everlasting love; Therefore I have drawn you with lovingkindness.

Psalm 13:5

But I have trusted in Your lovingkindness; My heart shall rejoice in Your salvation.

Proverbs 15:17

Better is a dish of vegetables where love is Than a fattened ox served with hatred.

Proverbs 13:24

He who withholds his rod hates his son, but he who loves him disciplines him diligently.

Cords

Cords are made of astral and etheric energy and connect two people's subtle bodies. They stretch between two people very much like an umbilical cord and transfer emotional energy and chi between the two. It does not matter how far away the other person is, as the cord is not a physical substance and distance is irrelevant, so it is still effective from the other side of the planet.

All babies have a cord going from their belly to their mother after the physical umbilical cord is cut. Some may have extra cords going from the heart, solar plexus or even the head to various parts of the mother's energy body. The cord or cords that exist during infancy last for a few years and gradually drop off as the child becomes more independent from the mother and does not need the connection any more. Well ideally this would be the case, but here on Earth so many people have emotional issues that very often the cords can last well into adulthood. The cord is supposed to be there to support the baby but in actuality many mothers are emotionally needy and actually use the cord to nourish themselves from the baby's fresh and abundant energy. Of course this is subconscious and the mother is not really meaning to do this. The baby is usually quite aware of what is happening and will even give the mother extra energy and emotional support through the cord at will. The baby is a very pure and loving being at this stage with only a small amount of astral incarnation and very little ego structure so they want to do all they can for the mother.

Unfortunately, as the baby grows up it gradually loses its perception of such metaphysical things and so forgets about the cord. The transfer of emotional energy becomes subconscious for the child as well as the mother and continues to operate for possibly a very long time. Cords between mother and child that last for prolonged periods often cause serious friction between the two parties leading to dysfunctional feelings toward each other.

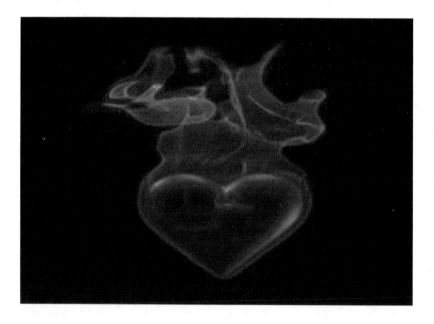

The relationship will suffer as there is bound to be resentment and negative feelings. Imagine you have been drained of energy by your mother for 20 years through a cord that has become thick and gross with negative emotions and emotional neediness. You do not know exactly what is happening but you sense that somehow you are being drained by her. You move to another country to get away but wherever you go it almost feels like she is there with you - she is draining you from afar. This situation is just an example; there are many ways to interact through a cord.

Another common cord is between two lovers. Each wants to share their energy with the other and during sex this is amplified greatly. The feelings of love and sharing are often enough to build a cord. Often these cords are between the bellies but can be in other areas like the heart or solar plexus, etc. So when two people have been in an emotional relationship for a time there is a good chance that the two people have a cord. Depending on the emotional issues of the two, the cord can become gross or can stay fairly clean and be a good thing which helps the two with emotional nurturing.

If one partner is needy it is likely that they will drain the other which could eventually lead to resentment by the drained partner. Some cords that become too gross can cause serious problems for a couple and could certainly lead to a break-up. Clearing a cord can help alleviate the emotional intensity so the couple can progress to a more balanced relationship. If a breakup does occur, the cord may stay for a long time and continue to operate, making it hard to let go and to move on with another partner. In this case clearing the cord can do wonders.

Cords can be created between any two people or even groups of people that have emotional relationships. Friends, workmates, enemies can all have cords. They can be used by entities and other dimensional beings to connect with us and drain our energy. It is possible to send a cord to someone you don't know if you really want to get to know them. For example, say you fall in love with someone but have not yet talked to them. It is possible that your desire to have them may send a cord into their energy. It is also possible to consciously create a cord to another person but this is in the domain of black magic witch work. You should never go to a psychic they use as means to purposely control you or affect another's energy without their permission. This is demonic and satanic.! If you have ever gone to one no matter how long ago you need to break and burn the cord in Yah Jesus name.

There are many types but whatever the case a cord is basically a connection between the astral and etheric bodies of two or more beings which allows for an exchange of emotional and or etheric energy.

Fortunately, all cords can be cleared fairly easily. It only takes one of the people to clear the cord and it will be cleared from the other. You can become aware of all your cords and learn to clear them. Interestingly while exploring a cord you can remember when and how it was created, how you felt about it and how it has been operating while it was there. Often cords can be seen and felt very tangibly and their effects become very apparent and can be dangerous to the soul if not broken from ex-lover old friend's exspouse or one night stands etc. If not broken it can also hold marriage back a delay and can cause you to reunite with an ex you have no business with. This is why many people cannot get over an ex and move on. The cord is there and if not broken over a long period time it gets stronger. The spirit demon and incubus succubus uses these people for a cord is lying there for them to see in the spiritual realm.

What Are Soul Ties?

A soul tie is an emotional bond or connection that unites you with someone else. You can become chained or bound to a person through your soul, which is made up of your mind, your will, and your emotions. It comprises what you think, what you want, and how you feel.We all have soul ties, whether good or bad, and understanding them is vital to enjoy the life God has for you. I truly believe you are destined to read this letter today because it will help you or someone you know that needs freedom.

Soul ties are formed in three ways:

(1) close friendships

(2) vows, commitments and promises made to each other, and

(3) sexual intimacy.

Know this, the more intimate you are with someone, the tighter that soul tie bond becomes and the more entangled you are to their soul. Satan works tirelessly to entangle you with the wrong person for a reason because he knows how damaging it is and how difficult it is to break free. Also it can stop your destiny and kill you as well before your time. Even take your soul to hell. Social media has become one of Satan biggest tools to connect people. Many times affairs come from new relationships build from online, but more often they developed as a result of reconnecting with past friends or lovers. *Satan can only use the old and our past to trap us.*

Attaching yourself to wrong soul ties can lead you to:

- *Destroy your marriage*

- *Lose the respect of your children*

- *Forfeit the plan of God for your life*

- *Feel dirty, used, sleazy, worthless, insecure*

- *Remain with someone just because of what you've done with them*

- *Experience deep regret*

Soul ties are very much responsible for the pain we feel when a relationship ends. Soul ties have deceived many young people looking for love, married adults flirting with disaster, and abused spouses trapped in a vicious cycle of torment.

"Keep me from the snares they have laid for me, and from the traps of the workers of iniquity" (Ps. 141:9, NKJV).

Satan and his demons are constantly knocking on the door of your heart looking for any entrance into your life (*and mine*). Once you open the door to him through your unguarded thought life, the battel begins! You are in a war! It's a war for your life! It's not a war that you can see with your eyes or fight with your hands-it's a spiritual battle.

Do not forget Satan knows you're not going to knowingly fall into sin. He has to deceive you trick you into thinking it's something good, something you need, not anything that will harm you. Deception is really simply believing in a lie and he is the father of all lies. Satan is incapable of telling the truth. *He could not even if it Pimp slap him in his lying face!!!* Someone whose life is veering off from God's path is spending more time listening to lies than truth. Just as God strategically brings good relationships into our lives to form healthy soul ties, Satan always brings counterfeits ones into our lives to form unhealthy soul ties. He will present people to you and say, "This is what you're missing sweetie!

Take a slice it won't hurt this time If you find yourself in this position today, God wants you to wake up! Enjoy and embrace everything you already have. God can make up the difference in any area you are lacking. Satan will do his very best to convince you that you cannot live without them until you're willing to give up all that you do have for something you don't have. In the end it will cost you more than you could ever imagine. Have you found yourself tormented by thoughts about a person, excessively wondering about them, checking on them, or remembering times with them? This mean a soul tie and cords need to be broken. Especially if they showing up in your dream's. **_You have soul ties_**. Have you grieved over a severed relationship with someone you were once close to? You have soul ties.

Do you miss them, long for them, desire to be with them? You have soul ties. You might ask, "What's so wrong with flirting with a little sin?" A little sin is like being a little pregnant. Sooner or later, it will reveal itself. Whatever gets in your mind and stays there for a period of time it takes root in you. It will eventually for show up in your life. Or we could say whoever is on your mind and stays there will eventually show up in your life. If you know you are in a wrong relationship with someone and God is instructing you to end that relationship, just know this. You give Satan rights to you. You just disobey God by not following suite of the relationship Life is not over when a relationship is. There is so much life for you to enjoy!

Read God's personal note to you (from Psalms Now: Psalm 23):

The Lord is my constant companion. There is no need that He cannot fulfill. Whether His course for me points to the mountaintops of glorious joy or to the valleys of human suffering, He is by my side. He is ever present with me. He is close beside me, when I tread the dark streets of danger, even when I flirt with death itself, He will not leave me. When the pain is severe, He is near to comfort. When the burden is heavy, He is there to lean upon. When depression darkens my soul, He touches me with eternal joy. When I feel empty and alone, He fills the aching vacuum with His power. My security is in His promise to be near me always and in the knowledge that He will never let me go!"

God loves you and He will never let you go!

Take hold of this promise from God to you! He is not angry at you. He loves you just as much today as He always has and will. His love is not dependent upon your past performances. He loves you because He is Pure love. God and all of Heaven are cheering you on desiring that you will wake up and embrace the joyous life He still has prearranged for you.

Now every love relationship could be called "impossible"

At one time or another, but here we're talking about love that's really impossible: An infatuation for someone you've never met or talk too or someone who's happily married, or someone who's not even slightly interested in you. **(Impossible love is an exceedingly** common and painful experience. **ESPECIAALY FOR teenagers, they** are not taught to wait to fall in love when they are of age and know God. So they can never get the right mate for their life and happiness and most important their destiny. Marriage is 90 percent of one destiny many don't even know this.

Many people are swallowing in pain because of broken heart's for loving the wrong one God has not chosen for them. Also must adults, may be full with guilt about their disloyalty to the real-life partner who has been eclipsed by our fantasy romance. Romance novel are really good to read. But let's face it they are just that romance fancy novel. Why do you think so many people read them and they are number one seller in books and movie? Well it is simply because people are just looking for love. So if they cannot find it in their own life they look for it in other. It's a mind over matter thing. Sinking oneself in other people fancy and love, to cover their pain or whatever they are missing in their own love life and marriage and relationship.Even worse, people are likely to be told that it is some textbook case of some psychological syndrome (as when we fall for a therapist, teacher, or minister–a phenomenon that psychologists call transference). "It's all projections" is a standard piece of advice. Or we might be told that "It's just something temporary that everyone goes through." No its called missing piece in your heart and plain all pain and finding ways to heal. The heart is desperate to be love in all kinds of faucet. If the heart is not loved, it really does not feel loved. Especially if you don't have God in your life. His love supper passes all love one may be missing in one life. His love fills up your heart Then there is no room from loneliness depression and pain. Because when pain comes he heals it and removes it when you cannot.

Mistakes one makes in looking for love and falling in love.

1-developing the discipline and grit needed to keep going even in our most hopeless moments

2-learning ways to show our devotion to someone who don't love us back.

3- not exploring our own hidden mysteries with in us what God place there for your mate.

4-creating an image of the kind of person we might fall in love with for real someday

5-intuiting a sense of the grandeur and possibilities of life

When you do these five things it is in my opinion disastrous. You don't give God a chance to for fill you and your heart and life and destiny with who he wants for you. You set yourself up for a life of pain and heart ache if you leave your love life in your hands without God hands in it.

Mankind has Hidden within them unfulfilled yearnings in mankind discovery one as human being is important—even if it's only to one selves—and that one is capable of loving another person—even if the current object of our desires doesn't know one exist.

By its very nature, impossible love has to change over time. It can't settle into a routine the way two real-life lovers sometimes do. Hidden from our awareness, the truths we discovered continue to evolve and to shape our lives as the years go by. It may be true that much of what we honor in our grown-up selves was first learned while we felt helplessly entrapped by the fiery and unfulfilled passions of impossible love.

Emptiness: A Doorway to the Fullness of Life

Emptiness is very universal: People knows those nagging saying Is this all there is? feelings. Us human fret about the fact that that we have made the wrong choices and missed our destiny. Those longago promises of love and fulfillment, Aim going to make you the happiest person in the world. Have now turned in to dust, and dust is exactly what we feel in our mouths, our hands, and most for sure our hearts. The heavy oppress feeling with the sense of wasted time and lost opportunities, really seems to have little spiritual meaning. However, though if you read traditional spiritual
literature, you will discover that emptiness had great value in that essence of times, because the empty space was believed to make

room for God. Detachment from all desires, possessions, and achievements was considered essential to union with the divine.

The fewer feelings you had–the more remote your heart felt from yourself and the people and things around you, the higher your spiritual state.

That road to spirituality has, thankfully, fallen into disfavor. Dispassionate, mechanical living has no value for us today: We want deep connections with others and a life that is rich in meaning. And mankind does not want God. God always tell me mankind of this generations today is a **MIROVAVE ONE.** Want everything to vastly meaning fast. Human being's. Don't want to take time to wait and pray to him and see what his stake is in one love life. marriage and future and destiny. But the old-time emphasis on emptiness has such a long history that it might be worth another look. Is there any value to the soul in those flat, cut-off, dead-end feelings?

Perhaps there is.

*Emptines*s opens us up to life's possibilities. When life is busy and full, it's natural to stop searching. But emptiness awakens our hearts and souls by reminding us that something more is waiting to be discovered.

Emptiness is an equalizer. It's impossible to feel arrogant when you think your life has no meaning. By stripping away our egos, emptiness strengthens our bonds with other people.

Emptiness strengthens our courage. Those flat, nothing-is-worthbothering-about feelings can drive us toward risks and new possibilities.

Emptiness sharpens our focus. Because we feel removed from ordinary concerns, we're able to concentrate on the rumblings within–and we're more likely to discover the kind of life we really want.

All of this requires, of course, the ability to sit with the emptiness, listening and tasting and smelling it until we discover what we truly want. Our misfortune is that contemporary life offers so many distractions that it's easy to give in to the temptation to smother those empty feelings. This puts us human's in touch with who we really are and what is really happening in our life. This should lead one straight to God. However not always.

We don't have to sit on a zazen cushion like a Buddhist person who don't really know God at all. they are truly lost ones that need to find the true path of the Real God. They sit the Buddhist at five o'clock every morning in order to befriend their own emptiness. If one look you can find countless opportunities in our daily lives to take a deep breath or two, feel the emptiness, and gently ask what it is hungering in us that need to be full up. Emptiness heals emptiness; feeling drained and lost teaches us how to feel purposeful and fulfilled.

But what do I do about I You Say?

Here are two suggestions for getting started: (confusingly, they contradict each other–but such are the mysteries of soul):

1. Commit. If a relationship, job, or activity triggers emptiness, try investing more time and energy in it. Would it help to set aside an evening every week to strengthen a foundering relationship? Could you undertake a new project at work? Greater involvement can sometimes bring renewal.

2.Withdraw. People change, and what you found immensely satisfying five years ago may not be working for you now. Is it time to end a relationship, make new friends, explore new activities, make an appointment for career counseling, or move to another location?

Understanding Enter Emptiness

No matter if we as human's are pouring our hard earn energy into the empty space or gently saying goodbye to what we once thought or found there, the actions we take of listening and movement are ways to honor our soul and at the same time, enrich our daily lives. Does anyone ever want to feel empty inside? It sounds like a nutty question. We've all experienced those pains' within, and we don't ever want to go back that way again. Who would willingly choose emptiness when life offers us boundless opportunities for fulfillment? So it's always a surprise to delve into traditional spiritual literature and discover that the saints of old positively craved emptiness. Their spiritual practices aimed not to fulfill their inner passions, but to silence them through self-flagellation, fasting, and solitude. Success was defined as a state of total detachment from the highs and lows of everyday life and love.

Today we shake our heads in disbelief that anyone would choose to live that way. Or do we?

It's true that spiritual practices have drastically changed—so much so that self-inflicted suffering is usually considered a sexual disorder rather than a pathway to spiritual growth. But it's also true that we value a certain kind of inner emptiness just as much as our spiritual forebears did. Think how often you hear the word *"addiction" clue to mankind's ear today, and think also of how much we as mankind* _**value words like "balance" and "serenity.**_ "Healthy people don't have cravings and passions, and they don't carry things to extremes— or so we are endlessly told_. **WHAT A LIE**_ So us folk's supposed to bounce back ever so rapidly after a broken heart or the loss of a loved one. The person who devotes hours, weeks, and years to an artistic or intellectual pursuit or an unconventional lifestyle is a good candidate _**for therapy—or so we think.**_

I'm not denying that genuine addiction is a very real problem for many people. No smart person would take that position. But it's also true that deep fulfillment in any arena requires time, energy, and (in many cases) money. Truth to tell, it often looks like obsession or addiction. In his book I once read that it takes at least 10,000 hours to attain world-class status in a complex skill or advanced field of knowledge. _**That works out to almost three hours**_ _a day, seven days a week, for more than nine years._

**And so I think that it Is surly possible that the way we look at** _mental health—a well-balanced life, no extremes, no excesses—is_ _**actually making really making us sick?**_ To say it in a nut shell. Perhaps we need to redefine what it means to be healthy and alive. Maybe should stop being so frightened by the roaring in our souls and the crazy ideas in our heads.

**We need to say NO to balance and serenity and YES to passionate living in God.**

**Way's To Make the Godly Choices when face with Life Issue.**

Ten Irrational Beliefs

**1-I need the approval of others in order to be happy.**

2-A person who behaves badly should in a relationship should get help.

3-I should not be terribly unhappy when something goes wrong.

4-If I avoid thinking about a problem, it won't go away by itself.

5-I can't face life without help from someone bigger, smarter, stronger, or better God.

6-If I make a mistake or fail at a something, I shall be extremely upset.

7-I will not be held back by negative things that happened to me in the past.

8-I cannot be in control all the time.

9-I cannot be happy without taking an active role in getting the life. God want s me to have I and I want as well.

10-When I experience a negative emotion, I can't do something

about it I can pray about it

The Language of the Soul

Language exerts hidden power, like a moon on the tides.

language is such a useful and familiar part of our lives, we as human being's tend to underestimate its importance. Language is way more than some small tool to communication, for it has power to organize our values and interpret our lives. The inner parts of ourselves—*ego, spirit, and soul*—speak in different languages. With good practice we can learn to distinguish between them, just as we might be able to identify a UK England or Spaniard accent. Knowing the difference between an ego impulse, a spiritual inspiration, and a soulful feeling of yearning can help us make thoughtful decisions in our everyday lives.

Ego Language

Ego is the conventional self that we present to the world, and ego language is the idiom of everyday life, concerned with management, achievement, security, coping, and getting it done. Ego strength is vital to everyday life: Without it we simply could not function effectively. But when ego takes complete control of our lives, we lose touch with a vital part of ourselves.

Ego Language   Soul

Language security   risk control

yield concept image manage

surrender power   courage

strive accept

strong   weak

sure uncertain

Spirit Language

Although we usually associate the word spirit with religion, we may encounter spirit language in any setting that focuses on personal growth and self-improvement. Spirit language can often be heard in support groups and therapy sessions, and it's frequently used in self-help books.

Spirit language is important because it lifts us up and connects us to a set of higher values. But there is a shadow side as well, for spirit language can diminish the soul, with its urgent call to explore the darker unknown parts of our being. Spirit Language Soul Language peaceturmoil unity disorder ideal real

higher   deeper

conviction doubt solid

unstable

Soul Language

You may already have learned that negative soul words *such as weak, turmoil, unstable* always seem to outnumber positive ones *such as deeper, courage, unity*. The Soul brings both gifts and challenges—vitality and joy when our deepest needs are met, and fear and uncertainty when we are called to explore our unknown mysteries. Soul conflicts often erupt when we are paying too much attention to ego needs such as *conformity and popularity* at the price of true intimacy and a deeply meaningful life. Similar problems can arise when the spirit becomes too powerful: The flight upward causes us to jettison vital parts of ourselves. Invariably the soul will call us back with dark emotional moods, uncontrolled passions, and other reminders of our need for connectedness and meaning. Now you can see this process firsthand in the spiritual journals of holy men and women.

During this searing process we come to a true understanding of humility. It is not, as so many think, a public confession of our mistakes and foibles. True humility begins with the discovery that in order to satisfy our soul's yearnings, we must give up the illusion of our own virtue and power. Good and evil exchange places as we

honor not the best parts of ourselves, but the deepest, darkest, and most embarrassing.

Soul and Others

Shifting values and reordered priorities of an awakening soul inevitably lead to changes in our relationships with others, so that a new problem arises. How do we make a bridge between our inner lives and the bigger world around us? Soul and ego have different ways of viewing the world. The ego's natural tendency is to place a blur between boundaries between self and society. If I'm unhappy, I assume that others are to blame, and I have the right to punish them. It's easy to see this in families Mother or father are unhappy, and it must be the family's fault, so everyone in the household really suffers. If a parent is always **_angry, anxious, or depressed_**, this pattern may persist for years, so that no one can ever remember a joyful holiday celebration or a fun-filled vacation. If God is not allow to step in

Sadly, many people never learn the first important lesson that the soul can teach us. There must be a boundary **between our inner and outer worlds**. Whether our feelings are negative **_rage, depression_** or positive **_love, religious faith_**, we must put a space between thinking and acting. We cannot assume, as so many always do, that there is something godlike about our feelings that gives us permission to impose on family, friends, and colleagues. This does not mean that we can withdraw into passivity, or that we should spend all our time trying to figure out what past experiences shaped our personalities. What soul demands is that we learn how to articulate our experiences in words, not actions, until we are confident about putting soul values into action. Developing this confidence and discernment is a challenge that we will face for the rest of our lives.

Impossible Love: then Hope Gets Left Behind

Almost every love relationship could be called "impossible" at one time or another, but here we're talking about love that's really impossible: An infatuation for someone you've never met, or someone who's happily married, or someone who's not even slightly interested in you. Or in love with someone who will never love you back. Even worse, we're likely to be told that we arte a case of some psychological syndrome as when we fall **_for a therapist, teacher, or minister–a phenomenon that psychologists call transference_**. It's all projections is a standard piece of advice. Or we might be told that It's just something temporary that everyone goes through.

Well why does it feel so real?

It means that a man a woman and a child simply needs God to make it and live through love, to survive it live it and breath through the breath of God, we must learn that without God no love can stand or even exist. Any love without God in it, it will not work at all. Why do you think rich famous people get married so much and watch partners in marriage? They don't have nor know God. There is something Hidden within our unfulfilled yearnings it is the discovery that we are important–even if it's only to ourselves–and capable of loving another person–even if the current object of our desires doesn't know we're alive. God place it there

By its very nature, impossible love has to change over time. It can't settle into a routine the way two real-life lovers sometimes do. Hidden from our awareness, the truths we discovered continue to evolve and to shape our lives as the years go by. It may be true that much of what we honor in our grown-up selves was first learned while we felt helplessly entrapped by the fiery and unfulfilled passions of **_impossible love. Impossible love is possible in God_**

Happiness Isn't Always a Choice Is

happiness a choice?

Sometimes.

The happiness is a choice slogan is so universal that it can seem crazy to even question it. In dealing with the ups and downs of my own life, I've often found it a useful tool for getting back on track after a disappointment or a mistake. It is hard at times bouncing back from disappointment without God, this is a proven reality. THIS IS also a very good reasons why ***happiness is a choice it*** is not a good slogan for the way we live our whole lives.

The fact is that fury things that can happen when we focus all of our brain matter on choosing to be happy. We fill up all the complex and wonderful mysteries ***inside us–dreams, secrets, images***, wispier of feelings and memories–into a big, lowly triangle, with the conscious mind–the part of ourselves that makes choices–on top. To give it to you more simply Instead of swimming around all the wondrously strange things hidden in our souls, we try to focus all our hard energy into making a choice.

This capacity to choose is very empowering and important, but it's only a small piece of who we are, and it shouldn't be our pilot all the time. At its best, life offers us so many multiple options, some of them are very scary. When things go wrong, because they do that is reality, it may be time for some serious soul searching and a wide brand new quest for new options and choices. Break off a relationship? Go back to school Change careers? Move? Start/Stop going to church? Look for professional help? Begin or stop a new project etc.!!.

If we decide that gritting our teeth and excepting the choice of happiness is the answer to every problem, we may not mess up the real courage to take the difficult steps that lead to genuine fulfillment. Of course happiness is a choice can be a useful tool, but only if we know when to apply it—and when not to. Faced with an emergency or a disappointment beyond or out of our control, the happiness-is-a-choice of a mantra that can remind us to look for ways to make the best of a situation.

The unhappiest people I've ever known have been total failures at this, sinking into gloom any time things didn't go their way. I use to be one of them before I let God in. Happiness is a choice even if you choose God to live for you still must choose to be happy in him no matter what life and the devil throws at you. There will always be Problems with relationships, jobs, families, and lifestyle choices. However, changing this and slimming theses issue down to barely none, may require drastic changes in one outlook and behavior—an especially scary prospect when the image we've polished so diligently is in for some fighting battling and scratches.

It takes courage and humility to admit that what worked yesterday isn't working today, and to stop trying to plaster over the cracks that keep showing up beneath the serene visage we've worked so hard to perfect. And—an even harder truth to accept—attaining real happiness can demand much more effort than we ever expected. I've often thought that "Happiness is a commitment" might be a much more useful mantra than the endlessly repeated ***Happiness is a choice theme*** Listen the good news is that a divine path and discoveries await us, along with new opportunities to connect with fellow travelers who have embarked on the same journey. And maybe, without realizing it, we'll be fire blazing a pathway for someone else who needs to take that scary first step toward an amazing life.

Example of What can Happen When the enemy uses Greed AND Love to take a Soul.

WHEN WE ALLOW THE ENEMY TO CAPITALISE ON OUR WEEK SPOT.

All of us have got our weaknesses and they are what the ENERMY targets all the time, because they can become the open doors for the principalities of darkness to get at us if we fail to have them blocked.

Let's look at the case of Judas Iscariot; A case of Greed

Matthew 26:14-16 NIV

Then one of the Twelve—the one called Judas Iscariot—went to the chief priests and asked, "What are you willing to give me if I deliver him over to you?"

So they counted out for him thirty pieces of silver. From then on Judas watched for an opportunity to hand him over."

Findings-

Judas Iscariot had a short coming of greed for money, he never did what he needed to do to ensure they this door was closed and remain closed. So the demon of greed was having a field day with Judas Iscariot.

Because Judas Iscariot was now controlled by the principality of darkness, he did whatever Satan wanted like a drunkard but soon enough his eyes cleared up when it was too late.

Scripture- Matthew 27:3-5

When Judas, who had betrayed him, saw that Jesus was condemned, he was seized with remorse and returned the thirty pieces of silver to the chief priests and the elders.

I have sinned, he said, "for I have betrayed innocent blood." "What is that to us?" they replied. "That's your responsibility." So Judas threw the money into the temple and left. Then he went away and hanged himself."

Findings

The devil scored big time with Judas Iscariot, now the veil was off and he is left standing there with a massive SIN beyond words and Judas went for round two of sin by taking his own life.

HOW TO PROTECT YOURSELF FROM THE ENERMY ATTACK

Our Lord savior and redeemer Yah CHRIST JESUS said it all in this passage of the scriptures - Matthew 26:40-41 Then he returned to his disciples and found them sleeping. Couldn't you men keep watch with me for one hour? he asked Peter. Watch and pray so that you will not fall into temptation. The spirit is willing, but the flesh is weak.

Power of Love Over Lusts

So many believe that they are just experts in love. I think God takes that spot.by miles and mountains he is the most expert of all. Listen Love comes naturally. Life show's us that this is not true. Love, however, is God's divine gift originating from Himself. God is love. Man's understanding of love is very limited even somewhat perverted at that. God's love's, however, has no constraints. In this sense of *Galatians 5:22-23,* Love against such things there is no law Like light, love freely stretches outs its arms.

The Godly Man

God's love is intensive.

Nothing can stop the penetration of the rays of God's love. We see this most clearly in the sending of His only begotten Son Yah Jesus Christ into the world to die for sinners. Here is love. God first loved us. Hope, love and joy all comes from God's good intention to help us in our miserable state of life at best. God doesn't need love he is love. However, the rest of us live on the flow of divine love which first floods our souls like an ocean dept. and then pours out into the lives of others.

Love and Feelings

Divine love is known for giving while man's concept of love is limited to his feelings and passions of lust. They think love is a feeling originating from good vibes coming from another person. Love, for them, equals attraction. Attraction for them, no matter what the basis, serves as their authority of certain intimate touches, talk and glances. Today sodomy, adultery, fornication and even divorce are all legitimized by this ungodly sense of love. With it, all is permissible; without it, all former commitments and relationships can be instantly forgotten. The mutual attraction for many serves as a god that gives them guidance to ignore parents' advice, pastor's counsel, and common sense. This god is their passion and feelings.

God's love gives rise to the other Great Commandment, to love one another.

Mankind will not and cannot, love one another without God's mighty love. Without God's powerful love, we are nothing without just the walking dead. We are created to love but however we cannot. A careful study of I *Corinthians13,* the Bible's great 'Love Chapter,' will clear all confusion as to what true love is. This were you will discover love's genuine motivation, characteristics and duration. Christianity does not stand on what people say but on what people do - whether they love one another or not. Love requires us to put the needs of others above ourselves instead of the popular view which equates love in mutual pleasure*. Did not God put the first born of heaven for us to live Yah Jesus.*

Love True Power

Love displays its true power when pleasure is totally taken away. How does one perpetuate his kindness, care, gentle talk, noble deeds, etc. when the object of his love becomes violent, cold, harsh, unloving and very ungrateful? Here we discover the glorious and noble power of God's love which breaks through our resistant, prideful, arrogant and dark hearts. Only God emblem of love can stop and change this. This why we see red hearts all over the world For it was the pouring forth of the blood of Yah Christ that effectively sealed God's love into our lives. The heart is Yahushua Jesus blood bleeding for us from the heaven's pouring in to our heart's here on earth.

FUNCTIONAL DEFINITION OF LOVE

Love is the commitment to care for others without respect to their response.

Put me like a seal over your heart, Like

a seal on your arm.

For love is as strong as death, Jealousy is as severe as Sheol; Its

flashes are flashes of fire, The very flame of the LORD. "Many

waters cannot quench love, nor will rivers overflow it;

If a man were to give all the riches of his house for love, It would be utterly despised."

For Woman

Men Who Can't Love Because they Don't Have God in there life.

By Graham Reid Phoenix in Relationships

It's important to know and consider men who can't find love, who can't love a woman.

Man's Love Jonesy's an overwhelming emotion you have about another person, an emotion that you can't truly explain nor understand but you can't seem to get rid of. It makes you want to be with that person, and hold tightly on to them, touch them, have sex with them. It shows itself as an exchange of energy, a polarity, that unites excites your soul. Love makes you feel wonderful and totally transforms life. Love is worship of the other person, the woman who is divine for a man or man for woman.

Love is the power house feeling behind our lives, it is the reason we mankind lives 'It is sad that so many men just don't feel this emotion called love, that there are so many men who can't love. Yes, they have relationships, get married, bring up children, but still their lives remain barren, they are still men who can't find true Godly love. They try hard but remain separated from their wife, or partner. They sometimes have co-dependent relationships that are based on need or filling inward emptiness, but they never truly know the wonder of an inter-dependent relationship based on trust and selfknowledge. Why!! They don't have God in them or their life at all.

What is it that holds them back? What is that gets in the way? What stops them?

Men Who Can't Find God or Love – Who Are They

1. Men who are looking for their mother.

I don't know whether the mothers or the men are to blame for this. The men are looking to be fed, have their cleaning done and be generally cuddle.

Lots of mother didn't really teach their son's to look after them self or care for woman.

2. Men who are too absorbed in themselves.

It's their life, their hobbies, their friends, their ambition, their children, their... Somehow their women don't seem to fit into the world of their equation. A man in this world since the beginning of times are used to running the world and filling their lives with activities and occupations. Nowadays men have even taken the role of father so seriously that they can forget that their woman is more than a mother.

He's out with the boy's forgetting his wife is waiting for him at home. He is not a Godly man. 3. Men who are on a mission.

The focus and dedication of a man on mission is an amazing sight. Sometimes it just goes too far. Sometimes the climber climbs one too many mountains and kills the relationship in the process, Sometimes the businessman goes on one too many trips abroad and loses sight of home. This a man on a mission to hell and taking his family with him. Why!! this is a man not guarding his spiritual cup nor his house hold.

Men need to find a spiritual balance in order to become a man who please GOD.

4. Men who see themselves as alpha.

These are the ones that cause me so much grief. They are men who have a misplaced idea about men needing to be the alpha-males. Yes, straight up animal's in nature wild ones at thast.do They don't have the intelligence a Godly man has at all. They have devil's in them for sure. They chase and conquer women to show how great they are. In the process they just show how lacking they are in any emotion, understanding or even humanity of GOD.

They MAKE THEM SELF no better than DEVIL'S IN THEM even if on the surface they appear to know what women want they really don't at all, These kind of men have been hurt greatly and hide it by hurting and conquering woman who don't know God or there self-worth in GOD.

5. Men who just want a pal Gal with French Benefit's Which only a Woman can give.

These are the sad ones who spend their lives going to the bar's strip joints etc. or the sports I game. They remember the great times with their pals when they were young and just want it to continue on. At times pal gal relationship work's it does not work when the woman becomes one of the lads, but this never lasts the woman gets tired and smartens up and see it for what it was, then the man is left wondering what happened.

Sometimes men just need to realize they Really need to grow up.

6. Men who are afraid of intimacy.

Men often have difficulty dealing with intimacy, particularly when a relationship appears to be out of their control. The interesting part of this is that men also have difficulty acknowledging that they have difficulty dealing with intimacy. They usually sublimate the emotions into actions that they can understand.

This can show itself as aggression or even abuse, but generally just results in sullenness and withdrawal.

Men who have this difficulty need help to overcome their fear and learn to become a normal part of the world.

7. *Men who want to be in Their Twenty again.*

This shows itself, in the mid-life crisis. Things were great when they were young, or so they remember. Life was free and easy, there were no pressures, no mortgages. Their women were beautiful and nubile in the time before children. They have affairs trying to reach their long lost nirvana. In the process they throw everything away.

It is possible, however, to bring your youth into your present life by changing your outlook.

8. *The Controlling Man.*

There are men who can't love who just never seem to get over the temper tantrums of their childhood. They want everything and they want it now. No-one is going to stand in their way. They lash out at their wife and children as well as their fellow employees at work. And friends and other's family member Nothing is good enough for them. They need to open their eyes and see that there is a big wide earth out there that does not focus nor revolve around them.

9. *Men who do not have polarity*.

These are the 'New Men' who feel compassion for their women and want to spend their lives honoring and worshiping them. There's nothing wrong with this as such but the problem comes when their masculinity disappears in the process. They go into 'their feminine 'and lose their sense of being a man. They seek equality with their woman and end up being the same. The polarity disappears and the relationship become empty. He is no longer the center of attraction.

10.*Mr macho man*.

This kind of man just get so tied up with being a man. They are handsome so very fine in suture, they drive a fancy car and they just expect women to fall over and drawl over themselves to get to him. Well at first they do. Then they find that there's nothing there, I mean nothing at all there's no substance, no real man at all. A man should not get caught in this trap, he should look at himself long and hard and slowly and look for what a woman sees in you.

Men, should take care, and become more aware of who they are and how women see them and how God see them too. Don't become one of those men who can't love a woman, be strong, be present and find love.

For Men

WOMEN CHRISTIAN MEN MAY NOT MARRY

.I have perceived among the youths, a young man lacking sense, passing along the street near her corner, taking the road to her house" (Proverbs 7:7-8).

1. The Unbeliever.

Scripture is replete with exhortations against such marriages (in both the Old and New Testaments). Contrary to popular misconception, God's prohibition against marriages to foreign women in the Old Testament was not due to racism. Instead, God was simply preventing the spread of idolatry. Israel, God's chosen people in the Old Testament, represented what Christians would later represent in the New Testament.

Hence, God's prohibition against marrying an unbelieving woman in the New Testament (2 Cor 6:14) is simply the extension of God prohibiting a Hebrew man from marrying a Canaanite woman in the Old Testament (Deut 7:3-4). "Do not intermarry with them. Do not give your daughters to their sons or take their daughters for your sons, for they will turn your children away from following me to serve other gods, and the LORD's anger will burn against you and will quickly destroy you" (Deut 7:3-4).What then, is a believer? A Christian essentially is someone who believes in the gospel of Yah Jesus Christ. What then, is the gospel? The gospel is 1. God is holy, loving, and just. He therefore, must condemn all sinners to punishment in the flames of eternal hell 2. You and I are all sinners who deserve nothing but God's wrath in hell after our deaths 3. God loved humanity so much that He sent His Only Son, Jesus (*__who was fully God and fully man__*), to die on the cross for your sins. Yahushua Jesus paid the debt for your sins and absorbed God's wrath on your behalf. 3 days later, Jesus resurrected from the dead 4. If you repent (turn from) all your sins and personally put your faith in J Yah Jesus Christ as your Lord, God and Savior, then you will have eternal life. (For more information on the saving message of the gospel, click here.)

2. The Divorcee.

Yah Jesus clearly taught that unless the first marriage ended due to a partner's sexual infidelity, a second marriage is to be considered invalid and adulterous (I explain this teaching further here). A divorced woman, therefore, is off limits for a Christian man— unrepentant adultery being a sin that prevents one from obtaining eternal life (1 Cor 6:9). "If she divorces her husband and marries another, she commits adultery" (Mark 10:12). "And I say to you: whoever divorces his wife, except for sexual immorality, and marries another, commits adultery" (Matthew 19:9).

3. The Older Woman.

Not a sin, but certainly not God's ideal. God expects men to be the spiritual leaders of the home (Eph 5-25) and it certainly requires an extra measure of grace to lead a woman who's older than you. Again, if you're a man and you're already in such a marriage, then honor it till the day you die—it's still a valid marriage and divorce is not an option! However, if you're not yet married but thinking about an older woman I want to remind you that God intentionally (with good reason!) created Adam before Eve in the First Marriage. Scripture informs us that God created man first chronologically for the sake of authority! (1 Timothy 2:12-13). Evidently, within the First Marriage, God intended chronology (age) to be a reason for authority. Apparently, even secular researchers are now beginning to discover results that back up God's wisdom as demonstrated in the Bible:

This is what I have learned and Read

If you're a woman two or more years older than your husband, your marriage is 53 percent more likely to end in divorce than if he was one year younger to three years older generally improves life expectancy, but the age gap between a couple affects the life expectancy of men and women very differently. Marrying an older man shortens a woman's lifespan, but having a younger husband reduces it even more, the study found.

Health records have shown previously that men live longer if they have a younger wife, an effect researchers expected to see mirrored in women who married younger men. However, a woman who is between seven and ten years older than her husband has a 20% greater mortality rate than if she were with a man the same age. *(Source* A new study shows that women who marry men seven to ten years younger than they are increase their mortality risk by 20 percent. This is the opposite of the finding for men who marry much younger wives – their life expectancy increases.

4. *The Feminist*.

There's no room within Christendom for the Christian feminist. Though women and men have equal value in the eyes of God (Gal 3:28), they certainly have different God-given roles. Any woman who tries to usurp her husband's authority or even claims to be a co-leader with her man is gravely dishonoring the God who created her to be subject and obedient to her husband (Eph 5-22, Col 3-18, 1 Pet 3-1). Eve was distinctly created "for" man, a point that the apostle Paul makes abundantly clear in 1 Corinthians 11 when he writes, "For man was not made from woman, but woman from man. Neither was man created for woman, but woman for man. (1 Corinthians 11-8-9). Men, your wife is to be your "helper" (Gen 218)–not your leader and certainly not your equal in terms of authority. Look for a woman who agrees with you in this very vital God-ordained relational dynamic.

5. *The Immodest-Dresser*.

 Being Sexy might catch your eyeballs, but it shouldn't catch your heart and carrying it away to lust hell fire. The way that a woman is willing to expose herself says much about her heart and **her. *And behold, the woman meets him, dressed as a prostitute, wily of heart" (Proverbs 7-10*). The text in Proverbs explains that a woman will dress in a certain way to catch a certain type of man. Don't be that man. Don't be the foolish man who's led by his hormones instead of the Holy Spirit. Remember you want godly, not racy.

6. *The Gossiper and Slanderer*.

Women love to talk, but there's wisdom in looking for a woman who speaks with wisdom. Gossiping and slander are not good things at all to have in your marriage. That old *show Desperate housewives* make for desperate husbands. Besides that, they learn to be idlers, going about from house to house, and not only idlers, but also gossips and busybodies, saying what they should not. Like it says (*1 Timothy 5:13).*

7. *Childbirth Avoider*.

A man should not marry a woman who is not willing to have children of her own. In the Christian worldview, there is absolutely no room for two married, biologically capable, human beings to remain intentionally child-less. Unless a barren curse is on them or one of them. And that curse must be broken off so they can bear children before God. If you are adverse towards having children, then there's a simple remedy for that single-hood. However, if God has called you to marriage, then He actually expects children. Both the New and Old Testaments are very clear on this teaching. Did he not make them one, with a portion of the Spirit in their union? And what was the one God seeking? Godly offspring" (Malachi 2:15). Yet she will be saved through childbearing—if they continue in faith and love and holiness, with self-control (1 Timothy 2-15).

8. *Wander-Luster*.

There's nothing wrong with the occasional vacation. There is something very wrong with a girl who regularly needs to be out of the home. The constant desire for new experiences, new places, new faces, and new forms of entertainment only serves to clearly manifest the fact that the woman has not found her rest in God at all not settle neither. Scripture speaks repeatedly about such women: **She is loud and wayward; her feet do not stay at home"** **(Proverbs 7:11)**; Besides, they get into the habit of being idle and going about from house to house. And not only do they become idlers, but also busybodies who talk nonsense, saying things they ought not to" (1 Timothy 5:13).

9. Career-first Woman.

I want to clarify something. There is nothing wrong with a woman who works (Acts 16:14), what's wrong is a woman who puts her career ahead of her family. Modern American society might hate to hear this, but God made men to be the providers and women to be the nurturers of the home (in most instances). It's okay for a woman to be a doctor, attorney, or any other professional. However, if her career is coming at the expense of her home, then something is wrong. If day-care is raising her children while she's at work, then something is wrong. I understand that there might be a season of life where the wife might have to be the main bread-winner due to her husband's unemployment, but it should not be the desired norm. The woman ought to be willing (and even desirous—to some extent) to give up her job for the sake of raising her kids in the Lord. So I counsel younger widows to marry, to have children, to manage their homes and to give the enemy no opportunity for slander" (1 Tim -5- 14).

10. Devotion-less Woman.

A virtuous woman must have, daily devotional time with her God? If she doesn't love the Lord now, chances are, she won't love the Lord after marriage. (Don't fool yourself–you're not going to change her.) No way no how if God cannot you cannot neither Men of God; You would want to marry a woman who has an intimate relationship with Yah **Jesus (not you)** Yahushua Jesus has to be the first man in her life then you . Here are some good questions to ask her for good reason save you lots of heart ache. Does she have an active prayer life? Does she have a heart for evangelism? Is she hungry for God's Word? What does her pastor think about her?

Do you remember this account from Scripture:?

Now as they went on their way, Jesus entered a village. And a woman named Martha welcomed him into her house. [39] And she had a sister called Mary, who sat at the Lord's feet and listened to his teaching. [40] But Martha was distracted with much serving. And she went up to him and said, "Lord, do you not care that my sister has left me to serve alone? Tell her then to help me. [41] But the Lord answered her, Martha, Martha, you are anxious and troubled about many things, [42] but one thing is necessary. Mary has chosen the good portion, which will not be taken away from her. (Luke 1038-42 Such women have picked the good portion, which will not be taken away from them. God be with you men. Strong families start with strong wives. Choose wisely and choose in the Lord!

What does the Bible say about dating?

The Bible has nothing specifically to say about single Christian women dating. In Biblical times marriages were arranged by fathers, but the Bible has some principles that would apply to that question. Here are a few:

Second Corinthians 6:14-16 tells Christians they are not to be unequally yoked with unbelievers Light has no fellowship with darkness." The way this would be applied is that Christians shouldn't date non-Christians.

The Bible tells Christians to keep themselves pure (1 Timothy 5-22) and to flee from sexual immorality, because their bodies are the temple of God (1 Cor. 6-18-20). So to keep yourself very pure, it's better to avoid being playful the wrong way and doing other things that arouse sexually. I'd suggest you' get to know a man for little while and seeking the face of God first as well and getting to know him before committing yourself to marrying him—for with God marriage is supposed to be for keeper. So if a man has a quick temper, cannot hold a job for long time, seems immature in various ways, criticizes or complains about other people, these would be some serious warning signs not to get serious with such a person. Ask the Lord for wisdom in discerning what a man is really like. **Proverbs 3:5-6** is a good Scripture for a young woman who would like to get a good Christian man: Trust in the Lord with all your heart, and lean not unto your own understanding. In all your ways acknowledge Him, and He will direct your paths."

THINGS THAT GET Singles In Yah Christ in Trouble and Satan Right's

Lie 1 You're single because you're...

You can finish the sentence yourself—just insert your adjective of choice. For me, it varies from 'fat' to 'ugly' to 'horrible', depending on the day. But I can think of so many friends who are beautiful in the world's eyes, who are lovely, funny, kind, delightful and single. So many. People of all shapes, sizes and personalities are single, and people of all shapes, sizes and personalities are married. What is attractive to one is not attractive to another. Shape, size, and personality are not why I'm single. In the Western world at least, more and more people are marrying later in life or not at all. I may be single, but I'm certainly not alone. This isn't because the human race is producing uglier or more horrible people, but because of a raft of social changes we've seen over the past century.

God is more powerful than our social situations, our looks, our personalities, and our insecurities."

God is more powerful than any social force or trend. The fact is that ultimately I'm single because God is in control of everything. He is sovereign. Likewise, those who are married are married because God is sovereign. Those who are widowed are widowed because God is sovereign. God is more powerful than our social situations, our looks, our personalities, and our insecurities.

Lie 2: God is not powerful enough to find you a husband or Wife

The older I get, the easier it is to believe this lie (which is closely related to the first). When I was younger, thinner, it was easy to imagine that God would send a husband along for me. Who wouldn't love me? I was wonderful back then! But the longer I remain unchosen (and that is how man in church make you feels), to make it to think that God's power can't reach this part of my life.

But I need to remember that in fact I am not unchosen. God himself has chosen me. And at the risk of stating the fact, if God can create the universe just by speaking (Genesis 1) if he can cause Pharaoh to let the Israelites go (Exodus 12) if he can raise Yah Jesus Christ from the dead (Luke 24) if he can use the purposes of evil men for his good purposes (Acts 2-2-24) if he can give us new life and change us from people who hate him to people who want to serve him (1 Peter 1) if he can, well, do I need to list every event in the Bible? If God can do all this, then he can find me (and you) a husband, easily. This doesn't mean "there's someone just around the corner for you, or that God will provide you with a husband. It just means that if you are single it's not because God is too powerless to marry you off to someone. It will come in good season when God's knows you and I are ready in Yah Jesus name

Lie 3: You're single because God does not love you

Most of us know this can't really be true. We know that God is love (1 John 4-8). We know he sent his own Son to die on the cross for the sins of sinful people. We know all that.

But have we stopped believing it?

Our world is decaying because of sin, and there is sickness, tragedy and sadness everywhere. We have all kinds of reasons to doubt God's love for us if the only thing we have to go on is what we can see around us. But we are such finite beings. We see so little. We "do not know the work of God who makes everything (Eccl 11-5). So we must look to the cross. The facts of the death and resurrection of Yahushua Jesus Christ are the same now as they were when we first believed. If God sent his own Son to die that horrific death in your place so that he can be in relationship with you, and if he did this while you were still a sinner (Rom 5-6-11), then maybe you don't need to doubt his love for you.

And if you cannot see God's love on the cross, why do you think you will see it in a man—especially a sinful man?

What happened are the Cauvery s is a much bigger and better demonstration of God's love than providing a husband."

What happened at the Cauvery iis a much bigger and better demonstration of God's love than providing a husband?

Lie 4: Because no-one has married you, you have no value

Many single women genuinely think they have nothing to offer. They think the fact that no man has chosen them for a wife is a reflection on them, and that it means they can't possibly have any value. I suppose it is just another expression of that age-old sin of thinking our value comes from how other people see us. At this point, Single people can offer the world around them a lot. Some single's think they do not matter. We single people can contribute to the lives of those around us. But that would suggest that our value comes from what we do, which is just as bad as thinking that our value comes from what other people think of us!

Someone marrying you will not make you valuable You cannot be made valuable, because you already are valuable.

Listen someone marrying you will not make you valuable. Doing things for other people will not make you valuable. You cannot be made valuable, because you already are valuable more than any Jewelry of diamonds and Gold are no price on you and me we are priceless and precious to God. You and me are valuable because God Almighty himself tenderly created you and me —in his own image, no less! You and me were valuable the minute God wrote yours and me days in his book (Ps 139-13-16), and nothing that happens to you or me in this life can change that. Only you and I can change it if we choose to leave God which I know I won't and I pray you the reader wont neither.

Lie 5 Getting married will fix all your problems

This is the lie that I fuse with the most. I know it isn't true to thinking There is actually no guarantee that marriage will fix loneliness. Some married people are incredibly lonely, trapped in awful marriages with no-one to talk to about it. And getting married is no guarantee that I'll never have to find someone to live with again, or that I'll be able to buy property and have more security. A husband might die soon after married or one's house might burn down. Those are tragic examples but even if things like that don't happen, I'm sure the picture I have in my head of what marriage will be like is probably very different from what it would actually be like. Paul doesn't talk about the anxieties and worldly troubles" of marriage in **_1 Corinthians 7_** without good reason. Yah Jesus' own disciples clearly recognize the difficulties of marriage. When Jesus tells them that whoever divorces his wife, except for sexual immorality, and marries another, commits adultery they say, If such is the case of a man with his wife, it is better not to marry" (Matt 19:9-10)!

**I'm not saying marriage is bad—as the apostle Paul would say, by no means! Marriage is a wonderful gift from God, and I'm absolutely delighted when my friends get married. I'd love to get married myself. But we must not fall into the trap of thinking that marriage will fix all our problems. It won't.**

Lie 6: You've got to find The One

This is the dumbest idea in the history of dumb ideas. Seriously. Thank you so much, Hollywood, with all the romper going on, for helping Satan blind us with this lie. While it is true that God knows whether we will marry and whom we will marry, there is absolutely no way that we can know. Unless God himself gives you a name or hands you a photograph, or a vision when you sleep, you just cannot know beyond a shadow of a doubt whether you've found the right one All you can do is pray, make a wise decision, trust God, and then be faithful to your marriage promises.

Don't look for 'the one'; instead, look for someone who produces the fruit of the Spirit. Look for someone who loves Jesus."

This is not to say you should marry any person as long as they're Christian, available. I'm also not saying there's no place for physical attraction and romance. What I am saying is this to you that in your desire to get married, don't look for the one instead, look for someone who produces the fruit of the Spirit. Look for someone who loves Yah Jesus. Learn from the fact that many in arranged marriages grow to deeply love each other and don't expect that you'll feel wobbly in the knees as soon as you lay eyes on your future husband. Ask God for a husband, but also ask him to change your desires so that you will be open to the advances of a godly man, should they come. As children of God, we are part of a massive family. The challenge for all of us, in our individualistic culture.

Lie 7: It's better to marry a non-Christian than stay single for life

God's family is huge, we're all sinful and sometimes we do a terrible job of loving each other. Singleness can be a very painful and lonely experience. Some decide it's better, in the end, to marry an unbeliever. Perhaps you are toying with this idea yourself at the moment.

Let me tell you, softly so you hear me It. Is. Not. Worth. It.

There are women married to unbelieving men. Some of these women did not become Christian until after they got married. Others were Christian and married a non-Christian. Others have watched their Christian husbands walk away from Yah Jesus. But not one of them would recommend choosing to marry a nonChristian while you still have a choice to make. Not one. Not the women who still trust Jesus, anyway. And here's why.

If you marry a man who doesn't know and love Jesus, here are your options:

You will eventually walk away from Yah Jesus yourself, as he becomes less and less important and relevant in your life and your husband becomes more important. And when you walk away from Yah Jesus, you will have exchanged heaven for hell. Or you will keep trusting Yah Jesus, but it will be difficult and lonely in at least some respects. There are men who left Yah and happy for their wife to go to church, and be happy for her and give money to church (as long as he can spend the equivalent on whatever he likes!), and he loves her. Being married to an unbeliever, it's about as good as you can get.   Every week the woman still goes to church without her husband. This is a very important part of her life with the man she loves. And, saddest of all, unless something changes between now and when her husband dies, she cannot look forward to standing with him before the throne of God in heaven for all eternity. He is going to another place. Or perhaps God will have mercy on you and save your husband once you're married. But when you marry a nonChristian I think you probably make it harder for him to take Yah Jesus seriously. Why would he, when you're not taking Yah Jesus seriously yourself? Of course, God is more powerful than your bad example, and he could still save your husband. But you have no guarantee that he will, and it's certainly not something you can demand. Given the previous two options, why take the risk? My dear sisters, if you are tempted to seek solace with a non-Christian, please don't. Don't even flirt with the idea.

It's dangerous to your soul for real!! Don't get into a situation where you will get emotionally involved and find it hard to think straight. Determine that you won't give in to this temptation if you don't feel the temptation right now and stick to your guns. Don't marry a man that his love is trying to persuade to abandon your moral convictions and live with him, or have sex before marriage because you think one night with you he will marry you. That is fairy tale thinking not logical Godly woman thinking. Responds by saying Laws and principles are not for the times when there is no temptation they are for such moments as this, when body and soul rise in mutiny against their rigor stringent are they, inviolate they shall be. If at my individual convenience I might break them, what would be their worth? Preconceived opinions, foregone determinations, are all I have at this hour to stand by; there I plant my foot.

Things to Know as a Single Princess of Yah Jesus Acknowledge your feelings

Admit your feelings are natural, but know that that doesn't make it right to give in to temptation. It's natural for women to be sexually attracted to men and vice versa, but just because it feels good doesn't make it right. Recognizing that you're attracted to someone can actually be helpful for avoiding sin because you know that, that person is a temptation. When you know that a man is a temptation for you, respond by asking God to deliver you from that temptation. But remember, there's no use praying 'lead me not into temptation' (Matt 6-13) and then putting yourself in a situation with the person you're attracted t

Practice good self-control

Listen if you are getting along really well with a non-Christian man and you are attracted to him in a romantic way, it's wise to pull back seriously you playing with hell fire you could get burn in more ways than you think. This might involve not hanging out with him as much as you have been, cutting down on texting, and calling not replying to emails or messages on social networking sites, We can control how intimate we become with people. The more time you spend with someone, the more intimate you'll become with them, with friendship quickly turning into something more. So exercise your self-control.

Rule Number One Don't flirt

Flirting: don't do it. Not only is it sexually immoral, it's cruel to flirt if you have no intention of entering a romantic relationship with a person

Dress modestl

What wear says a lot about you. If you're serious about obeying God's command to be sexually pure, you will dress virtuous. I mean not like granny. Just lovey and Godly. If you wouldn't wear an outfit to church because it's too risqué and racy, why are you wearing it outside of church?

1. Be accountable for Yourself

Make yourself accountable to another Christian regarding your sexual purity. Choose this person wisely. I think it's good to choose a Christian who scares you a bit—someone you respect. Meet regularly. Pray together. Do a Bible study about sex and marriage?

2. Maintain good friendships

When all else seems to be paired up, you can feel very alone. So it's important to keep close friendships with other women. Friendships with Christian men are great too if you strong in your walk with God and he is too. It not it is gasoline waiting to unite a fire you may not be able to put out. However, Satan might could. I think it's healthy and refreshing for Christians to treat each other as brothers and sisters in Christ, not as potential husbands or wives all the time.

3. listen Mourn your singleness

Do you believe that God's word says that you should only marry a believer, you think you may never get married? Thinking that you may never get married can be frightening and depressing, and it's incredibly frustrating when non-Christian men find you attractive and Christian men don't pursue you. However, you need to come out of your grief and enter a place of contentment. Some woman say to me they wish that they could be happy in their singleness, but God doesn't say you have to be happy; he tells us to be content. For some woman discontentment is about fear—fear that they will never get married, fear that their not going to have children, fear of being alone. God's word talks about his perfect love driving out fear (1 John 4-18). I think the love of Yah Jesus is the only thing that can calm one fears about remaining single. Discontentment is dangerous because it leads some Christians to date or marry unbelievers. However, although deciding to fix the 'problem' of singleness by dating and possibly marrying a non-Christian might solve some of the problems singleness brings, it will also create new problems.

4. Flee from sexual immorality

Don't get into situations where you're tempted to sin. In Genesis 39, Joseph literally runs away from another man's wife when she tries to seduce him. So if someone's trying to seduce you, run. Flee from sexual immorality. Every other sin a person commits is outside the body, but the sexually immoral person sins against his own body. Or do you not know that your body is a temple of the Holy Spirit within you, whom you have from God? You are not your own, for you were bought with a price. So glorify God in your body. (1 Cor 6-8-20)

9.Alway's Remember God

KNOW who is the one you're sinning against God. When David turns back to God after committing adultery with Bathsheba, he pours out his feelings and says, against you, you only, have I sinned (Ps 51-4). Thinking about Yahushua Jesus when you're in a tempting situation is a powerful incentive to keep yourself pure.

10. Repent

Flee sexual immorality? What if you fall sexually? If that happens, repent—turn away from your sin and take some comfort in the fact that you have been saved by grace, not works. You may still feel bad about your sin, but remember **Psalm 103:12: As far as the east is from the west, so far does he remove our transgressions from us.** Confess your sin to God and ask for his forgiveness. Being sexually pure doesn't just happen, like any area of godliness in our lives, it requires work. And like any sin, if you sin sexually, you need to flee to the Yah Jesus. When ONE IS forced to choose between satisfying the desires of the flesh and the heart by being with a non-Christian and being obedient to God, remember that God sent his Son Yah Jesus to die for you. Thinking about Yah Jesus and the blood he shed for you, his resurrection and the hope of heaven is a great incentive to obey. When you say no to a romantic relationship with a non-Christian for Yahushua Jesus' sake, that pleases God. Life on earth is very short compared to eternity in heaven.

Boundary all woman should have

1. Setting a boundary is not making a threat

Setting a boundary is not making a threat – it is communicating what the consequences will be if the other person continues to treat you in an unacceptable manner. It is a consequence of the other person disrespecting your wishes. Setting a boundary shows that you respect yourself. Which is a critical piece of communication in the first 3 months of dating.

2. *Setting a boundary is not an attempt to control*

Setting a boundary is not an attempt to control the other person – although some of the people who you set boundaries with will certainly accuse you of that – just as some will interpret it as a threat. Setting a boundary is part of the process to define what is acceptable to you. It is a major step in taking control of how you allow others to treat you. It is a vital responsibility to yourself and your life.

Boundaries I think every single woman should have especially Godly Women

1. *Treat Your Sexuality Like a Queen*.

How would your sex life be if you were a Queen? Queens are precious to their community they rule with authority, control, and class. They govern their affairs wisely. They practice self-control. They know they are beautiful and worth the wait. They don't put up with lawbreakers and sniff neck men like the bible talk's about, and men who want to shirk their responsibility within their community. You can call me old-fashioned, but I think women need to build better boundaries in this area. Sex has become far too casual these days. Women actually have the power to inspire men to grow up and gain some self-control. But they're not.

And *THEY NEED IT.*

2. *Do not Stay in the Gray Forever*.

Woman deserve to be courted but you also deserve to be married (if you desire to be). If you've been hanging out in the dating ride far too long, make him take the biff off and be a man or get off the pot. No more stringing you along. No more being friends with benefits of acting like married. That's just messing with your heart.

And your heart needs to be guarded above all else. It's your strength in Yah of life. Start changing things up, by putting up a time boundary and see how he responds. Boundaries in courting before marriage are extremely important for a woman protection against manly temptation's

3. Use Your Honey to Attract Bees,

Not ant's or strange files or wrong bee's. Law of attraction, Crazy attracts crazy. What are you putting out there and communicating to the world at large? Sure we should celebrate women's beauty. But let's redefine public beauty. It's not your figure. It's character, face, story, and passions. A woman's worth is not found in her outward appearance, but in her heart. Do your actions, words, and appearance reflect that truth? How do you dress around men? How do you act around men? What kind of words do you say around men? Use your honey to attract someone who you want coming around, not some fly who wants something for nothing.

For a believer to marry an unbeliever is to sin grievously against God and God's people.

This is the message of Malachi 2-10-12. As we read the priests had failed to live and teach God's truth, causing many to stumble. From the contemporaneous books of Ezra (9, 10) and Nehemiah (13:2329) we see that one of the ways the priests had set a bad example and thus had led the people astray was in this sin of marrying foreign women who did not follow the Lord. In fact, they were even divorcing their Jewish wives to marry these foreign women (Mal. 213-16). Through the prophet, the Lord warns His people against the sins of marrying unbelievers and divorce.

1. For a believer to marry an unbeliever is to sin grievously against God.

Our text unfolds four aspects of this sin:

MARRYING AN UNBELIEVER IS A GRIEVOUS SIN AGAINST THE GOD WHO MADE US HIS PEOPLE.

Father may refer to Abraham, but probably it refers to God, who is the Father of the Jewish nation as His chosen people (1:6). He created and formed the nation (Isa. 43-1), not only in the sense that He created all people, but also in the sense that Israel was to be a special people for His possession. He entered into a covenant with the fathers of the nation, singling them out from all others on earth. As their all-wise heavenly Father, God has the right to tell His people whom they can and cannot marry. If you know Yah Jesus Christ as Savior and Lord, you are not your own. You have been bought with the blood of Yah Christ. You are only free to marry as the Lord directs in His Word. As I'll show in a moment, He does not leave room for doubt. His will is always that you marry a believer, not an unbeliever.

A-MARRYING AN UNBELIEVER IS A GRIEVOUS SIN AGAINST THE GOD WHO WANTS HIS PEOPLE TO BE HOLY (SEPARATE) UNTO HIM.

God is holy, meaning that He is totally separate from sin. He calls His people to be holy also (Lev. 19-2- 1 Pet. 1:16; plus, many others). Here the Lord charges Judah with profaning the covenant (2-10) and the sanctuary (2-11), literally, "the holy thing." This probably refers to the people themselves. God had said that He would dwell among them and they would be His people (Lev. 26-11-12). By marrying those who worshiped foreign gods, the Jews had defiled themselves as God's dwelling place. You may think that marrying an unbeliever is unwise, or perhaps a minor sin. But God calls it an abomination (2-11). That Hebrew word is used elsewhere to refer to idolatry, witchcraft, sacrificing children to idols, and to homosexuality (Deut. 13-14; 18-9-12; Lev. 18-22). It is not a gray area!

To underscore how grievous this sin is to the Lord, I want to take you on a quick tour through the biblical witness against it. The principle runs throughout the Bible: God wants His people to be separate from unbelievers in life's important relationships. Throughout history Satan has used marriage to unbelievers to turn the Lord's people from devotion to Him. In Genesis 6, however you interpret "sons of God," the point is the same.

Satan used wrongful marriage to corrupt the human race, leading to the judgment of the flood. In Genesis 24-1-4, Abraham made his servant swear by the Lord that he would not take a wife for Isaac from the Canaanites. Two generations later, the godless Esau married two unbelieving wives. It is emphasized repeatedly (Gen. 26-34-35- 27-46-28-8) that these women brought grief to Isaac and Rebekah. Later (Gen. 34) Jacob's daughter, Dinah, got involved with a Canaanite man. His people invited Jacob's sons to intermarry with them and live among them (Gen. 34-9).

Later, Jacob's son, Judah, married a Canaanite woman and began to live like a Canaanite (Gen. 38).If Israel had continued to intermarry with the Canaanites, it would have sabotaged God's plan to make a great nation out of Abraham's descendants and to bless all nations through them. So God sovereignly had Joseph sold into slavery in Egypt, resulting in the whole family of Jacob moving there, where they eventually became slaves for 400 years.

This drastic treatment solidified the people as a separate nation and prevented them from intermarriage with the heathen. Later, through Moses, God warned the people not to intermarry with the people of the land (Exod. 34-12-16- Deut. 7:1-5). One of the most formidable enemies that Moses had to face was Balaam, who counseled Balak, king of Moab, against Israel. God prevented Balaam from cursing Israel.

But Balaam counseled Balak with an insidious plan: Corrupt the people whom you cannot curse. Get them to marry your Moabite women. The plan inflicted much damage, until Phinehas took bold action to stop the plague on Israel (Num. 25-1-9). Throughout Israel's history, marriage to heathen women created problems. Samson's ministry was nullified through his involvement with Philistine women (Judges 16-4-22). Solomon's idolatrous foreign wives turned his heart away from the Lord (1 Kings 1-:1-8). The wicked Jezebel, a foreign idolater, established Baal worship during the reign of her weak Jewish husband, Ahab (1 Kings 16-29-22:40). Jehoshaphat, who was otherwise a godly king, nearly ruined the nation by joining his son in marriage to Athaliah, daughter of Ahab and Jezebel (1 Chron. 18-1). The terrible effects of this sin did not come to the surface during Jehoshaphat's lifetime. His son, Jehoram, who married Athaliah, slaughtered all of his brothers and turned the nation to idolatry. God struck him with disease and he died after eight years in office.

His son Ahaziah became king and lasted one year before being murdered.Then the wicked Athaliah made her move. She slaughtered all her own grandsons (except one, who was hidden) and ruled in wickedness for six years. The Davidic line, from which Christ would be born, came within a hair's breadth, humanly speaking, of being annihilated because of Jehoshaphat's sin of marrying his son to an unbelieving woman (1 Chron. 17-1-23-15)! After the captivity, when Ezra heard that some of the returned remnant had married women of the land, he tore his garment, pulled some of the hair from his head and beard, and sat down appalled. This was followed by a time of national mourning and repentance (Ezra 9 & 10). Just a few years later.

Nehemiah discovered that some Jews had married Canaanite women. He contended with them, pronounced a curse on them, struck some of them, and pulled out their hair, calling their actions a great evil (Neh. 13-23-29)! One of the priests had married the daughter of Sanballat, one of Nehemiah's chief enemies in the project of rebuilding the walls of Jerusalem. Malachi's ministry fits into Nehemiah's time or shortly after. The New Testament is equally clear: Do not be bound together with unbelievers; for what partnership have righteousness and lawlessness, or what fellowship has light with darkness? Or what harmony has Christ with Belial, or what has a believer in common with an unbeliever? Or what agreement has the temple of God with idols? For we are the temple of the living God (2 Cor. 6-14-16a).

When Paul gave instructions for those in Corinth who were married to unbelievers (1 Cor. 7-12-16), he was not endorsing entering such a marriage. Rather, he was giving counsel to those who had become believers after marriage, but whose spouses had not. In 1 Corinthians 7-39 the apostle gives a clear word concerning entering a new marriage: "A wife is bound as long as her husband lives; but if her husband is dead, she is free to be married to whom she wishes, only in the Lord" (emphasis mine). My point is, there is a principle that runs throughout the Bible: God wants His people to be set apart unto Him. This especially applies to the major life decision of whom you marry. It never is His will for His people to join in marriage to unbelievers.

Thus for a believer to marry an unbeliever is to sin grievously against the God who made His people, who calls them to be holy.

C. MARRYING AN UNBELIEVER IS A GRIEVOUS SIN AGAINST THE GOD WHO LOVES HIS PEOPLE.

Judah has profaned the sanctuary of the Lord which He loves (211). Remember the theme of Malachi, "I have loved you," says the Lord (1-2). It is because of His love that God sets forth such strong standards of holiness for His people. Sin always causes damage. Holiness brings great joy.

We often forget that God's motive behind all of His actions toward us is, He loves us! We're like rebellious children, who don't want to eat nutritious food or brush our teeth. So we run away from home, where we can eat all the junk food we want and never brush our teeth. After the first few days of this freedom, we defiantly say, See, I'm still healthy, my teeth haven't rotted and fallen out like my mother said, and I'm having a great time! My mother was wrong! Just wait! Satan always tempts you with the promise of immediate gratification and the lie that God really doesn't love you or He wouldn't keep you from all this pleasure. Here's how this works: You know that God doesn't want you to marry an unbeliever, but then the most adorable hunk asks you out. You hesitate, but then rationalize,

What can one date hurt? Besides, your phone hasn't been ringing with Christian guys asking you out. So you say yes, you'll go out to dinner. You plan to witness to him, but the opportunity just doesn't come up. You're pleasantly surprised that he isn't a rude, crude pagan, as you'd been led to think all unbelievers would be. He's a decent, caring, sensible young man. So you go out again and again. Then, there's a polite goodnight kiss at the door. Your feelings for him are growing stronger. The kisses become more passionate, and they feel good. You feel loved and special. Soon, your physical involvement has gone too far and your conscience bothers you. But you brush it aside, thinking, "He's going to become a Christian and we'll get married. It will all work out.

At the start of this subtle drift away from God was your rejection of God's love, as expressed in His commandment for your holiness. As a Christian, you need to make an up-front surrender of your life to God, trusting that He loves you and knows what is best for you. That includes His commandment for you not to marry an unbeliever. If you don't want to go to the altar with an unbeliever, don't accept that first date.

D. MARRYING AN UNBELIEVER IS A GRIEVOUS SIN AGAINST THE GOD WHO DISCIPLINES HIS PEOPLE.

God's love is not incompatible with His discipline. In fact, it stems from it: "Whom the Lord loves, He disciplines" (Heb. 1-:6). If I love my child, when he does wrong I will correct him strongly enough to deter him from taking that course of action again. In verse 12, there is a difficult phrase, translated, everyone who awakes and answers being awake and aware, or whoever he is. It is probably a Hebrew idiom meaning everyone. So the verse means, whoever sins by marrying an unbeliever, whether he does it defiantly or ignorantly, may he and his posterity be cut off from the covenant people of God." God often lets us experience the natural consequences of our sins. The man who marries outside the faith is, in effect, thumbing his nose at God and God's covenant people. So, God declares that he and his descendants will be cut off from God's covenant people. It's the principle of sowing and reaping. If you sow wheat, you don't reap peaches. If you marry an unbeliever, generally, you won't have children who are committed to the Lord. They will see your halfhearted commitment, seen in your disobedience in marrying an unbeliever. They will also see the pleasure-oriented, materialistic lifestyle of the unbelieving parent. They will conclude, Why commit myself fully to the Lord?

Thank God, there are exceptions, especially when the believing parent repents. But no one should disobey God and hope for their case to be the exception! If the believing partner thinks that he (or she) can disobey God and then "bring his offering to take care of things, Malachi says, Think twice! Such offerings will be of no value. God looks for obedience, not sacrifice. Your children will suffer for your disobedience.

This leads to the other part of Malachi's message. For a believer to marry an unbeliever is not only to sin against God. Also,

2. For a believer to marry an unbeliever is to sin grievously against God's people.

We never sin in private. Our actions are interwoven with the fabric of society. If we defile our part of the fabric, the whole fabric is affected. Malachi states that God's people are one (2-10). To sin against God by marrying an unbeliever is to sin against our brothers and sisters in God's family. It's as if we're all in the same boat and you think that you have a right to bore a hole in your part of the boat. What's it matters to you how I live in my part of the boat? you ask. It matters a great deal, of course! There are three ways that you hurt other believers if you marry an unbeliever:

A. IF YOU MARRY AN UNBELIEVER, YOU CHEAPEN GOD'S COVENANT IN THE EYES OF HIS PEOPLE.

Malachi asks, why do we deal treacherously each against his brother so as to profane the covenant of our fathers? (2-10). The Hebrew word treachery is related to their word for garment or covering. The idea is that treachery involves deceit or cover-up. To marry foreign women covered up Israel's covenant relationship with God. When one Jew saw his neighbor act as if there were no such relationship, he would be tempted to act in a similar manner. That's why I maintain that for a believer to marry an unbeliever should be a church discipline matter. If a believer marries an unbeliever and there are no consequences of being put out of the fellowship, then lonely believers in the church will think, she seems to be happy, but I'm still lonely. No Christian guys are available. Maybe I'll date some non-Christians like she did. A little leaven leavens the whole lump" (1 Cor. 5-6).

How to have a long lasting love relationship and Marriage

Chemistry

The reason why relationships have chemistry or passion in the beginning is for two main reasons. Polarity and proximity. When two people have close proximity to each other combined with an aggressive "masculine" and an open feminine energy (polarity), you have a recipe for passion. If you want magnetic chemistry, make sure there are opposite energies at work to create passion. When men and women come at each other with intensity and control the magnetism is compromised. Men, stay focused and protective. Women, allow yourself to be open, receptive and relaxed.

To build something meaningful

Commitment to building a family, having children or participating passionately in community help to establish a unifying purpose. It makes marriage less about just the two of you and more about building something together. Selfish love transforms into selfless love when you can, as Stephen Covey says, begin with the end in mind".

How can you create, or recreate the spark?

What you see is what you're going to get. If something about your prospective spouse bothers you, but you think that you can change your beloved after you're married, you're wrong. Be prepared to live with whatever bothers you—or forget it. Your spouse will undoubtedly change during a long marriage, but not in ways you can predict or control. Grow together. Make decisions as a team. Be willing to let your partner pilot.

Consideration

This one sounds obvious, but be considerate and caring. Just be nice to each other! Wish for your spouse to flourish and be successful. As the years go by, tension and anger start to build naturally. The key to making sure anger doesn't turn into contempt is constant care and respect One way to practice respect is to listen to your spouse using active listening skills, body language and verbal cues. Here is a thoughtful article written by Elizabeth Bernstein with common sense tips on how listening creates intimacy, mutual respect and the feeling of being really seen and heard by your partner.

Love Play.

Be spontaneous. Laugh more often. Do fun things together. Share in life's adventures. And finally, spend time as often as possible remembering why you came together in the first place.

When you get right down to it, marriage it is not about happiness. Marriage is about two people growing up and becoming better humans.

Nowhere else are we faced with the task of growth more than marriage.

So what's the secret to making marriage last?

Two people who choose to stay married. That's it.

Marriage is choice. Choice of partner, choice of self, choice of growth, even choice of passion and adventure.

While this may at first appear simplistic, it should be.

When you view what's going on in your marriage as a process for growth and experiencing more in life, it makes the choice simple.

Most of the time, we focus on our partner and our desire for them to change or do something different. This is focusing on something we can't control. If we decide to grow, do something different, change the things we don't like about ourselves, we take charge of our own life as well as our relationship.

With everything that happens to us in life and love, how you view it will determine the outcome. When you have times of disagreement, could it really be a time to grow closer? Or a time to understand more about your spouse? When you feel your partner pulling away, maybe it's an opportunity to engage your partner in a better way.

Why Do Demons Oppress Women More Than Men?

This verse is used frequently by people to say that humans can't have sex with 'angels'. But why? Upon closer investigation, the verse does not say this at all. It says that ANGELS OF GOD IN HEAVEN do not marry nor are given in marriage. In Jesus' own words, He clearly specified the angels of God in heaven. He is not talking about demonic fallen angels. Nonetheless, one of two things happened here in Genesis 6:

(A)   *the fallen angels had sexual relations with the women, and the women then gave birth to the Nephilim/giants. Or,*

(B)   the fallen angels somehow genetically implanted their serpent seed into these women, thus using them as a host in which to birth their corrupted race. Is it possible they were not attracted to them sexually speaking; rather, these women met their qualifications for the bringing forth of their demonic race?But what does this have to do with the headline, you ask? It has much to do with the headline.

Women, since the beginning of time, were the doorways to corruption in the human race. Does this mean woman are evil, or that women can't be used of God? Heavens no! I am not implying that women are any different than men when it comes to wickedness. What I am saying is that because more women tend to be ruled by emotions rather than facts (not all women, but MORE women), women can oftentimes be more receptive, or open, to demonic attacks than what men are.

Men and women alike, since the fall of man, are both hunted, stalked, and tormented by demonic entities. In fact, just as God assigns angels to us, Satan assigns demons to us as stumbling blocks to persuade us, lure us, and pull us away from God. Whether we are possessed or oppressed, they will be there to try and get back in as long as we live in a body of flesh. This is why it is important to keep all the doors in your own spirit securely shut! You do this by accepting Jesus as your Savior, obeying God, staying in His Word, communicating daily with God, fellowship with other believers, and actively practicing spiritual warfare each and every day against the enemy—rebuke him using God's Word and the name of Jesus all throughout your day.

However, when we give place to the enemy in our life, we are willfully opening doors into our spirit and letting him walk right in.

A Christian can't be possessed, as to be possessed means to be owned. One who has invited Yah Christ into his or her own spirit to dwell can only be oppressed. To be oppressed is no different than to be possessed, except that the victim is not owned because they have been bought with the blood of Yah Jesus Christ. Sometimes, whether we are oppressed or possessed, we require deliverance. Certain demonic spirits are more difficult to get rid of than others, but they can be cast out.

In regards to a specific type of demon the disciples had no success casting out, Yah Jesus said, in Matthew 17:18-21,

18 And Yah Jesus rebuked the devil; and he departed out of him: and the child was cured from that very hour.

19 Then came the disciples to Jesus apart, and said, why could not we cast him out?

20 And Yah Jesus said unto them, Because of your unbelief: for verily I say unto you, If ye have faith as a grain of mustard seed, ye shall say unto this mountain, Remove hence to yonder place; and it shall remove; and nothing shall be impossible unto you.

21 Howbeit this kind goeth not out but by prayer and fasting.

Men and women alike are emotional beings, however, as I've mentioned above, women are naturally more emotional creatures than what men are. That is how God made us, to complement one another with our strengths. Where a woman lacks, the man complements and vice versa. As a result of sin in this world, men and women disagree, argue, fight and even split up over these differences daily—the very differences God intentionally created, yet Satan, once again, has corrupted.

This is one of the main ways Satan has broken down society as a whole—through the family! Sadly, it is oftentimes us women who lure men, whether through acts of lust, seduction (what we wear, how we walk, talk, gesture, etc.). The enemy is well aware of this and will use us to tempt men, (who are supposed to be the 'spiritual' head of the household—the God figure of the home, spiritual leader) into sin in order to destroy the family.

When he can get in and attack the family, he can get in and manipulate and destroy the body of Yah Christ, society, school systems, media, pervert every family and moral value there ever was, and much more! This is the plan. That is why we are seeing less moral values, less family values and more corruption than ever—homosexuality, adultery, fornication, domestic violence, abortion, crimes against children, addiction, hatred, strife, etc. Overall, there is a great amount of moral decay, and not just on a national level, but on a global level!

According to the Spiritual Science Research foundation, in 2012, 70% more women were affected by demonic entities while only 30% of men were affected. But how can we put a number on something like this? I believe just about everybody is oppressed or possessed by demonic entities. However, I do agree that women may very well be more of a target due to their emotional nature, and we can see it in the Bible with Adam and Eve, as well as with the daughters of men and the fallen angels. The woman was targeted firsthand by Satan himself—he went through the woman first to get to Adam!

This needs to be known by all who are married and Will get married of the lord and Hopefully bring people to lord. This will surely scare you to God and get you right in Marriage or Get you married for God after Reading This.

SEXUALLY TRANSMITTED DISEASES: THEIR WITCHES CONNECTION

The devil has three basic ministries i.e. to kill, to steal and to destroy. Witches are human being who gives their spirit and soul to the devil (by entering into a covenant with him) and because of this devil use them as agents (report and bring human beings to devil and its evil spirit) to meet out evil and even kill human beings. Whenever they close their eyes to sleep they are off on their evil errand for the devil. Their spirit and soul can move easily through the air (looking as if they are dreaming i.e. spiritual) to attack their human victims in form of birds (when they are sleeping). Witches meet in the coven (assembly of witches) every night (12:00 midnight).

They make human beings captive. If your spiritual level is very low they can arrest and take the spirit of that person captive in the night and from there affect all his or her activities and even kill him or her. In their coven, spirit of human captive looks like animals e.g. goat. Anything they do to that animal representing your spirit in their coven, it will affect you physically. Whenever they kill the animal in their coven the human captives will die later. Witches can travel (spiritually) in a split second to any part of the world to attack their victims. This is because they move through the air and there is no barrier in the air. Witches press people at night to suck their blood. In the night they normally turn to animal like cat, wall gecko, cockroach, owl e.t.c to met out their evil designs. Witches uses incantation (words use in magic spell), invocation (summon up by magic), manipulation (operates, handle a person with skill or craft), seduction (convinced or tempt somebody to do wrong especially physical sexual intercourse or sex in dreams), divination (discovery of the unknown or the future by supernatural means) and enchantment (charm, magic spell) on their human victims.

Moreover, spirit of witchcraft and their evil spirit knows about this law that when vaginal secretion (women) or semen i.e sperm and other secretions (men) comes out of your body through masturbation or any other normal or abnormal sexual practices, sexually intercourse, wet dream, homosexuals etc the sexually transmitted micro-organisms (STM) i.e. bacteria, virus, protozoa, yeast like fungi will be in its favorable period (because the body physiology , science of the normal function of living things especially animals and body biochemistry branch of science that deals with how living things are made up, how they combine and how they act under different conditions are now lowered) to reproduce and multiply and comes back (or even be more than) to its former number.

The witches can also monitor person that is not spiritually strong (don't pray, don't read the Bible with understanding, don't claim the promises of the Bible, don't live a holy life, don't fast e.t.c.) and by enchantment and divination in the night direct him or her to a person carrying sexually transmitted diseases or any other communicable disease who he or she must meet when he wakes up and go out in the day. Sexually transmitted diseases (even Aids) can never be contracted spiritually (through wet dreams). When you get these diseases (especially sexually transmitted diseases, leprosy, tuberculosis e.t.c) the first thing they will do is to send one demon (spiritually) to monitor you 24 hours and report to them. Their work this time is to induce or cause you to be looking anyhow to the opposite sex, (the eyes is the door to the heart, the heart considers it, the brain will start to describe it) and also incite (cause to happen by one's actions) you to think about the opposite sex, women or men as the case may be. They will now make you to be lusting i.e. to have violent desire to possess something especially strong sexual desire (lust of the eye, lust of the mind, lust of the flesh). In the night the witches and evil spirit always work with what you stored in the mind or heart during the day.

When they come in the night and find out that your mind is feel up with sexual desires, they will then by enchantment and divination bring the opposite sex (man or woman) to you in dream and you have no other option than to have sex with the person (i.e. wet dreams). This is because they will induce you into it and base on the fact that your mind is filled up with sexual desires you will go into the act unwillingly. But when you are conscious of this and deal with your eyes, mind, and body this lusting will be reduce to a minimal or minute extent.

Now when you walk on the street you don't look anyhow (or have second or third look) on women faces, breasts, buttocks or their shapes. When you look at all this features of women it will induce you to arouse (awake sexually) and consequently leads to lusting. If a woman or a girl looks anyhow on men it will make them to arouse and consequently lust over them. A man of God said that if you don't want to sin when you are walking on the street you look straight and don't look at any human being (opposite sex) twice even when your mind instructs you to do so. Lust-free life brings your spiritual level to the highest point while lust-filled life brings your spiritual level to the lowest point.

More so, the evil spirit can also bring in news of women or men (as the case may be) and sex into your mind (the battle field) and induce you to start to think about them. All human beings have this evil presentation in their mind but the difference between a true believer and unbeliever is that when it comes into the mind of a true believer, he or she will reject it and cast it out but when it comes to an unbeliever, he will start to consider and think about it which will contaminate (dirty) the mind leading to lust of the mind. Once the devil brings this views of sex, women or men (as the case may be) to your mind quote the word of God. Bible (sword of the spirit) to him in your mind without speaking it out.

You can tell him that the Bible says in proverbs 4:23: guard your mind with all diligence because from it flows the issues of life, you can also meditate on 1 peter 2:11 beloved I beseech you as aliens and exiles to abstain from the passion of the flesh that wage war against the soul. Once you are quoting this you are reminding the devil that you know the consequences of those things he presented to you for consideration and he has no option than to fly away. You can also cast it out by saying Holy Ghost fire on it without saying it out officially. Once this is done the devil will fly away and your mind will have peace. Moreover, God hate sin and don't have much to do with a sinful body. You cannot overcome sin with your human power but if you accept Jesus as your personal Lord and savior he will then give you the grace and power to overcome sin. Devil has tested heaven and he doesn't have any other chance of being there and so he is utilizing the entire spiritual and physical weapon at his disposal to prevent man from making heaven.

Nevertheless, when you defeat them in lusting (lust of the mind, eyes and flesh) in case of a person with sexually transmitted diseases (STD) the witches and the evil spirit has the power to invoke out sperm out of your body through the penis when you are sleeping in the daytime or in the night. When your spiritual level is low, you can see the sperm physically when you wake up but when your spiritual level starts to increase you will feel the ejaculation while sleeping but when you wake up you won't see the sperm, but ejaculation of sperm whether seen or not will lower your body physiology

A science of the normal function of living things especially animals) and body biochemistry (i.e. branch of science that deals with how living things are made up, how they combine, and how they act under different conditions) and make the disease to start afresh because the sexually transmitted micro-organisms i.e. bacteria, virus, protozoa, yeast like fungi will have favorable period to reproduce exponentially (very rapidly or quickly) by binary fission (i.e. each bacteria, protozoa, and yeast like fungi divides itself into two parts and each of the two parts divide into two parts and the division continues, and stop when the physiology and biochemistry of the body comes up to normal again.

They later grow into new bacteria, protozoa, yeast like fungi respectively) or by replication (i.e. reproduce or make exact copy of itself continuously and stop when the physiology and biochemistry of the body comes up to normal again) in case of virus. You can stop this attack entirely by constant, fervent prayer and unquenchable faith. You can also add flavor to prayer and faith by turning your face and body down to the bed (prone or prostrate) and cross your leg while sleeping so that they won't enchant directly on your penis or vagina. The witches and evil spirit has the power to cause and worsen any disease in any person that is not spiritually strong. An eminent evangelist, said that when you are sleeping and later wake up suddenly in the night, that you should know that a witch is about to attack you. When we pray before sleeping (on a background of holiness) we find out that spiritually you will be covered with fire and blood of Jesus and devil and its agent will find it impossible to get to your mind, body, soul and spirit because our life is now hidden in Christ and Christ in God Colossians 3:3. When they see that there is no way to enter your body they don't have any other option than to wake you up. When you wake up suddenly and fail to decree short prayer they will now attack you because your body is now open to them. So when we are having or treating venereal or sexually transmitted diseases or certain other diseases like stroke, pile etc.

We should know that when we wake up suddenly like that and did not decree short prayer before sleeping again, the witches and their evil spirit has power by enchantment and divination to multiply the sickness under this condition and make it to start afresh. That is to say that any time you are sleeping and wake up suddenly (no matter how many times you woke up before that time) make sure that you decree short powerful prayer (binding the devil) which will then cover you afresh and the witches and their evil spirit will find it impossible to enter. Witches fight the prayer life of their victim to disconnect them entirely from God.

This will make them to be totally in control of their victim. Fear and anger hinders the presence of the Holy Spirit and give room for the evil spirit to have a free day. Devil put fear and doubt in your mind to destroy your faith which is your visa to heaven. Mathew 18:18 verily I say unto you, whatsoever you shall bind on earth shall be bound in heaven, and whatsoever you shall lose on earth shall be loosed in heaven. Luke 10:19- Behold I give unto you power to tread on serpents and scorpion and over all the power of the enemy and nothing shall by any means hurt you.

Ephesians 3:20- Now unto him that is able to do exceeding, abundantly above all that we ask or think according to the power that works in us. Albeit, the witches and evil spirit can also interfere into any disease (especially sexually transmitted diseases) that they didn't cause (i.e. it comes by human error or mistake) to worsen it and bring untold hardship and suffering to the victim and ultimately kill the person (after exhausting his or her money on the disease). Also you must know that nothing can chase away witches and evil spirit out of your life except you deal with yourself. Free yourself from lust of the flesh, eyes and mind (i.e. holiness), pray fervently, read the word of God (Bible) with understanding and (Faith) claim God promises.

Prayer shakes and renders devil and its agents powerless and stranded. Paul and Silas shouted their prayer inside the prison and that is exactly while other prisoners heard them and this was followed by a violent earthquake and later their release (Act 16:2526). The people of Israel would have walked round Jericho wall and the wall will fall flat on the seventh day after walking round seven times, but God told them to shout (Joshua 6:20). This shows that shouting has spiritual significance.

The prayer you shout out has more power than the whispering prayers (or shell ox prayers). So endeavor to shout while praying (solemn word to God). When you worship idol or have charm: something believed to have magic power, good (bring good luck a trinket worn on the body, and against evil spirit) or bad (influence people in a magic way), talisman: something that thought to bring good luck e.g. a trinket or ring, amulets: something worn in the believe or hope that it will protect the wearer against evil (which is of the devil).

God will never intervene into your case or hear your prayer not until you remove all the property of the devil in your life because he is a jealous God (Exodus 20:5). Native doctors, diviner, necromancer, fortune-teller, star gazers have no solution for witches and wizards because they are all from Satan and the Bible said that in Mathew 12-23 that a house divided against itself will not stand, so they can't help you at the expense (loss) of the devil their master. When you live holy and righteous life and you are spiritually strong you can see vision from God. No doubt, devil can also come with his fake or counterfeit vision but the spirit of God in you will help you to trace the source of the vision and how you will respond to it.

This vision is very important because it makes you to know about spiritual happening around you and your family and makes you to know where and how to direct your prayers but the vision you accept into your life must come from the Holy Spirit and not the evil spirit (Joel 2-28,29). By their fruits we shall know them (Matthew 716a)Killing of animals . sacrifice can't drive away evil spirit and witches but you can do so by cleansing yourself and doing the spiritual exercise as I underlined above.

While praying reshape your voice. The witches will attack you with that reshaped voice they picked and because of the fact that it's not your normal voice which is specific to you and have spiritual network (there won't be any spiritual network) the attack (manipulation) won't be viable and effective. Bind (Matthew 18:18) and destroy all the manipulation, enchantment, divination, incantation and network of the witches and wizards design to attack you through the air in the name of Jesus. When you pray believe that what you're praying for is already done (faith) and think positive. To fast in a body that has lusting, as foundation is meaningless and powerless. It is hunger strike. But to fast in a body that has holiness (i.e. without lusting) as foundation makes you powerful, spiritually and physically. Devil fears holiness because with it he can do nothing. Witches and their evil spirit can induce bad habits (drunkenness, drug addiction, truancy, homosexualism, womanizing etc) into a person with low spiritual level.

The witches can also take advantage of your weakness when it comes to sexual reproductive organs to deal with you; in short it is devil's major target because it is a sin against the body and brings down your spiritual level abruptly. Witches enter into human body through the head, when praying bind, the head and its top so that witches (and their consequent attack i.e. wet dream etc) will find it impossible to enter. Witches can bring weakness and tiredness when you're about to sleep to prevent you from praying. But don't allow them to succeed. Before you sleep make sure you pray and bind all their networks.

Howbeit, all this attacks of the witches and their solution, mention above are the experiences of one of my staphylococcus aureus male patient. The witches captured him when he was in secondary school. They inspired him to be practicing masturbation. This lowers his spiritual state and then made the witches accessible into his life.

He experiences series of motor accidents and sicknesses design by the witches to scuttle his academic career (i.e. by elusive memory – memory that forgets easily) and even kill him. The witches (evil spirit) later by enchantment and divination started ministering unto him spiritually that his problem will be solved when he meets a woman.

They later made him to meet a lady carrying staphylococcus aureus. Since that day he will be treating the disease while the witches worsen it both spiritually and physically. He pass through so many prophets, native doctors, orthodox and Pentecostal churches and pastors who sap (finish up) his money leaving his problem unsolved. By divine intervention he started hearing (and doing) raw messages on holiness, prayer, faith, restitution, fasting, the efficacy of the word of God. He is now dealing ruthlessly with the witches and on taking our drugs (Eminence consult natural medicine) the staphylococcus aureus vanished. He is now bouncing in good health. The size of your faith will determine the extent of God's presence in your life (i.e. your blessing). Your faith is like the sum of money you went to the market with, the more money you have the more goods (quantity and quality) you come out of the market with. John 8:32-And you will know the truth, and the truth will make you free.

A man of God that repented from the occult world said that the number of demons working for the devil is three times the human population of our egalitarian world. From this, we should know that devil mean business (he is not playing), so Christians must sit up. The witches and wizards can lock the brain and understanding (retentive memory) of an intelligent person, close your business if you are not spiritually strong.

The most precious thing in your life devil is fighting for is your great faith which is your visa to heaven. Ephesians 6:16-Above all, taking the shield of faith, with which you shall be able to quench all the fiery darts of the wicked one. Hebrews 11:6-But without faith it is impossible to please him, for he that comes to God must believe that he is, and that he is a rewarder of them that diligently seek him. Whenever you believe and have faith in the promise of God in the Bible, it works completely because his words are Yeh and Amen. The promise of God in the Bible is like a certified cheque given to you to clear from the bank, you rightly believe that the amount written in the cheque must be in your pocket when coming out of the bank. All your doings (good or bad) in this world is in your spirit. When you die, God will unroll it and judge you from there. Do your restitution (give back something stolen to its owner or expose all evil plot you executed against anybody and ask for forgiveness). No restitution no Heaven.

Secret worsen situation, expose it and liberate your mind. Heaven is a place of bliss and happiness and for you to make Heaven, you must be happy, stable and light within (in your spirit and soul) and without (your countenance i.e face including its appearance and expression and your behavior) in this world. At any moment in time, you personally know where (whether heaven or hell) you will go if you die because their criteria (standard of judgement) and benchmark (standard or point of reference) are clear and conspicuous in the Bible.

You don't need to die before you know where you're going, your heaven or hell starts from this world. When you want to sleep in the day or in the night go out and watch the position of the sun (day), moon, star (night). Take position on the bed and close your eyes. Thank God for sustaining you up to that moment. Remember to voice out your prayers. sun, moon and star are the storehouse (reservoir) of all satanic (negative) powers. In order to destroy this, focus (project) your spirit on the shining sun (day), moon, star (night).

You watch them before praying physically. Bind (sense it in your spirit) and destroy the powers transmitted through the shining sun (day), moon and star (night) against you (which can lead to wet dream). Bind, (sense it in your spirit) and destroy your voice picked physically by their human agent or your voice picked spiritually when you are talking in dream (which leads to wet dream). Numbers 23:23-No enchantment against Jacob and no divination against Israel (KJ 2000). Bind (sense it in your spirit) and destroy all manipulation, enchantment, divination, seduction, incantation (through the air) of the witches and wizard against you in Jesus name.

Remember to bind on top of the head. Witches enter into their victim spiritually through the head. When you bind on top of your head, witches will find it difficult to enter into you and their attack will be fruitless. Cover yourself, your room and your environment with the blood of Jesus (Revelation 12:11), then sleep. When you wake up suddenly don't mind to go out again to watch the position of the shining sun (day), moon, star (night). Just pray with the position of the shining sun (day), moon and star (night) you saw outside before you went to bed.

You do this while the eyes are still closed. Once you open your eyes when you wake up suddenly, go out and watch the position of the shining sun (day), moon, star (night) if you so wish before you pray or you can pray immediately and sleep without watching the position of the sun, moon and star again. While binding if you witness any spiritual resistance to the binding shake your head horizontally and faster.

This will overcome the spiritual resistance and paralyze the devil and his cohorts. After praying, sleep immediately, the power in the prayer will come down to barest minimum if you open your eyes again before sleeping. Putting Semen (sperm and other secretions) or vaginal secretion or only the name of a person you committed adultery or fornication (or any wrongdoing you committed together) with into a shrine or deity is not good it spoils your future and destiny. The shrine or deity don't have any direction (any bus stop), they move towards any direction depending on if divine (God's) argument (as written in the bible) favor them. Two of you committed adultery and fornication (or that wrong doing) together and the deity or shrine must follow two of you and spoil your destiny or future. So desist (cease) from it and shun (avoid) adultery, fornication (or any wrongdoing). Deity and shrine can't spoil the future and destiny of a righteous person (the person is on God's side) because they have nothing in common. Fornication (sex between unmarried man and unmarried woman), adultery (sex between a married person and another married person that is not his wife or her husband or married person (man or woman).

And woman or man (unmarried) respectively, Homosexualism: male (man) to male (boy) i.e. pederasty, male (man) to male (man), female to female i.e. lesbianism, incest (sex between near relations e.g. brother and sister, mother and son, mother and daughter, father and daughter, father and son), sodomy or bestiality (sex between human being and animal), sodomy (sex through the anus), masturbation (a situation whereby a person uses his or her own hands to bring sexual feelings to himself or herself, cannibalism (practice of eating human flesh by man) destroys the destiny or future of the persons involve, their marriage and their family.

Sexual perversions (abnormal or unnatural sexual habit) like homosexualism (i.e. lesbianism, pederasty, sex between man and man) incest, sodomy or bestiality, sodomy, sex with human corpse (dead body) especially in the mortuary, masturbation (and even cannibalism) are abomination and create a negative spiritual network (brings bad luck and poverty) that work against you as a woman and make you not to marry on time and can bring wrong husband to a woman (and even wrong wife to a man). If you are a witch and you want to be free from spirit of witchcraft, restrict or stop any way semen (male) i.e. sperm and other secretions or vaginal secretion (female) can come out of your body (i.e. through masturbation, pederasty, lesbianism, bestiality or sodomy, sexual intercourse etc).

Pray and practice spiritual solution as I underline above, (shun lust of the eyes etc). When you do all this, the spirit of God will come into your life and that spirit of witchcraft which has lesser power will varnish or disappear. When a man and a woman marry, they are now one (Genesis 2-18, 24) and have joint (one) destiny and future. Extramarital affair (adultery) destroys and perforates (put holes in) marriage and family.

Giving (offering, money or anything giving to anybody) especially tithe (Malachi 3:10, 11) open the window of heaven (material especially financial prosperity) and rebuke the devourer (devil and his agents) for your sake. The retaining (continue to hold) of semen i.e. sperm and other secretions (men) and vaginal secretions (women) makes you to be spiritually strong, while constant ejaculation or release of semen (men) or vaginal secretion (women) makes you to be spiritually weak.

The witches (including the spirit of witchcraft people manipulate physically through deity or shrine to attack people) and other evil spirit can manipulate your name (. your first name, second name and surname) to attack you spiritually (wet dream in men) or physically. Wet dream is an erotic (giving sexual pleasure) dream that causes unconscious ejaculation or release of semen. Sperm and other secretions. Witches use enchantment and manipulation to cause the multiplication of sexually transmitted micro-organisms when women have sex in dream. Witches can also manipulate you to urinate on your bed while sleeping. They use enchantment and manipulation to bring information to the mind of people (physically or spiritually) for consideration. Sand (land) is God's creation and it spreads evenly throughout our egalitarian world.

When you speak (through prayer) good or bad to the sand you are carrying on your palm (hand) and pour it out to the land again with faith, your statement will work out and affect the people (or situation) concern positively or negatively as the case may be. There is power in nature (sand) and in spoken words. Proverb 18:21 death and life are in the power of the tongue and they that love it shall eat the fruit thereof (KJ 2000). Job 22:28a that you shall also decree a thing and it shall be establish for you (KJ 2000).

You receive God's blessing anytime you attend church services (no matter the level of your sin). If witches discourage you to the extent that you stop praying, know that accidents, unusual sicknesses and death can come easily. Aids- acquired immune deficiency (or immunodeficiency) syndrome is a disease caused by infection with the human immunodeficiency virus (HIV) transmitted in the blood, semen and vaginal fluids and which destroys the immune system, leaving the body susceptible to potentially fatal infections.

Aids related complex (ARC) is a condition that manifest prior to the onset of full-brown Aids, characterized by fever, weights lose, thrush (internal inflammatory disease), shingles (skin disease forming a band of inflamed spots often round the waist) and a general feeling of malaise (feeling of bodily discomfort, but without clear signs of a particular illness). Aids or STD no defy shows for face, so hate and renounce sex before marriage. Aids i.e. Acquired immune deficiency syndrome is also a sexually transmitted disease, we have the cure and also give expert advice on how to live comfortably with it.

If you want to see more of this last subject you can go to The Source Read   more   at http://www.modernghana.com/news/255186/1/sexuallytransmitte d-diseases-their-witches-connec.html

Well this is the end of the book. This book is very educational for the saint's and non-saint's. By the time you read this book you will begin to have a better marriage and future marriage. Also to look for the spouse God wants you to have. ***AND BE SET FREE*** Most importantly love yourself and Most Importantly Love God and get real close to him. I give God all the Glory for this book in Yah Jesus name.

By Rosalind Solomon